Trail To Her Heart

by

ALYSIA S. KNIGHT

Heart Dreams PRESS

Trail to Her Heart
By Alysia S. Knight
Published by Heart Dreams Press
Copyright © 2015 Alysia S. Knight
Cover design: by Kelli Ann Morgan @
www.inspirecreativeservices.com

The views expressed within this work are the sole responsibility of the author and do not represent Heart Dreams Press or any of its affiliates.

This is a work of fiction. Names, characters, place and events are product of the author's imagination. Any similarities to actual persons, living or dead, business establishments or events are purely coincidental.

ISBN:1942000057
ISBN-13:978-1-942000-05-1

Also available from
Alysia S. Knight

Letting Love Win

 CRBO

Past To Die For

CRBO

Temperature Rising

CRBO

Kare for Me

CRBO

Blind Witness

CRBO

Beauty and the Chief

CRBO

His Governess

To those who are always ready for any adventure life throws at you. I hope you enjoy.

Alysia S. Knight

Chapter One

1859 West Virginia

Uneasy, Jessica Wellington looked around the mansion's hall. The evening didn't feel right, though nothing had felt right since her mother's marriage to Bradley Calloway.

Bradley never let anyone in the house. He kept her meek mother tucked away while he flaunted her wealth. Now tonight, a house party. Jessica didn't like it. Glasses clattered, conversations hummed as neighbors moved around in all their finery, but she felt alone.

Unable to take it any longer, she escaped out onto the veranda. The cool air and sweet smell of spring flowers calmed her. For a moment she felt peace, but it was shattered as a male figure moved out of the shadows in front of her.

Cruelness seeped from Clifford Raker as his cold, dark eyes traveled over her. His large body was dressed in the top of fashion, but he would never be mistaken for a gentleman.

"Jessica, how lovely you look tonight." He tried to make the words sound smooth but they grated over her nerves as did his use of her first name.

Jessica pulled back.

He stepped closer.

The sickening shiver she experienced every time she

saw him ran through her. When her father was alive, Clifford Raker was not allowed on Wellington land. Jessica shuddered again remembering the reason.

"What are you doing here?" She managed to force out.

"Now, that isn't any way to greet a guest." His voice dropped to a patronizing rumble.

"You're not welcome here." Jessica stiffened, trying to hold her ground.

"What would your poor, fragile mother say, hearing you talk like that? You know how she hates disturbing scenes. And besides," he moved forward until he towered over her. "Bradley invited me."

His dominating air frightened her. Jessica shook her head, though she believed her stepfather had indeed invited him. "He had no right." She took a steadying breath. "He might have allowed you here tonight, but don't expect it to happen again."

"Tsk, tsk."

"I mean it. In one month The Meadows will be mine. Bradley will have no say, and you will not set foot here."

"You've grown up into a lovely woman," he spoke as if he hadn't heard her. "Filling out nicely, like I always knew you would. You have such marvelous spirit. I like spirit." He leaned toward her, lowering his voice. "I like to bend it to my will."

Unable to believe he was speaking to her in such a manner Jessica remained frozen until his hand came up to touch her cheek, breaking her trance. "How dare you." She jerked away. "I want you to leave now or I will get some of the men and have you shown out." She moved to pass him.

He grabbed her arm with bruising strength.

"Release me!"

Instead, he tightened his hold, pulling her closer so that his breath slithered over her face as he spoke. "I couldn't be like Bradley, wanting a lifeless, compliant wife."

Jessica wanted to balk but knew it was an apt

description of her mother. Something had died in her when her father died, but Jessica refused to acknowledge it. "Release me!" She ground the words out.

"I want strength, fire, fight." His leer left no doubt he wanted her.

She tugged back, but he didn't release her, then to her relief a couple moved out of the ballroom onto the veranda. This time when she tugged, her arm came free. She hurried through the open double doors, knowing the man's gaze was still on her.

Jessica had no time to collect herself as the bell for supper tinkled the moment she stepped into the room. She joined the flow of people and moved to her seat next to her mother.

Bradley cut her off directing her to the other side of him as he pulled out her chair. Unable to ignore him, Jessica settled onto the edge of the seat. When a shiver of unease ran over her, she looked back. Clifford Raker stood behind her. A smug expression twisted his face.

"Clifford, there you are," her stepfather greeted the man. "Will you take your place?"

Jessica jerked around to her stepfather as Raker took the seat next to her. Jessica didn't like Bradley's smile any better than Raker's.

After a formal greeting, Bradley took his chair and they were served. Trapped between the two men she despised, Jessica found it impossible to eat though she gave a monumental amount of attention to the food she pushed around her plate. Jessica had just reached the point when she thought she could take in no more when Bradley tapped his crystal glass with his knife, sending it ringing for attention. He stood and cleared his throat.

"I have an announcement to make. I am sure many of you wondered about our gathering here tonight," he paused. "We meet here for a joyous occasion. I am pleased to announce the marriage of my stepdaughter, Jessica." He looked down at her, but she was too shocked to react. "To my good friend and neighbor Clifford Raker."

It took a second for the words to penetrate, but when they did, Jessica started out of her chair only to be pulled back down. Jessica's outcry of "no" was cut off by a wave of pain. Clifford gripped her hand under the table, bowing it backward until Jessica thought her wrist would break.

Tears welled in her eyes. Her refusal became a gasp of pain, but it too was muffled as Clifford wrapped his arm around her and pressed her face into his shoulder, shielding her from the crowd in what must have looked like an awkward hug.

Muffled against the unyielding body, Jessica heard her stepfather announce that the wedding would take place the next day at noon. She tried to fight back and scream her refusal. Clifford bent her wrist back further. Pain swamped her body. Lights burst in front of her eyes. She felt light-headed and nauseated.

"She fainted." Jessica heard Clifford Raker exclaim over the roar in her ears and then felt herself being hauled out of the chair and locked against his chest. Her face was pressed just above his pungent underarm, increasing the tears swimming in her eyes. The hold on her wrist fell away, sparing her more pain just as she slipped into oblivion.

೧೩෫೨

The first thing that registered on Jessica's mind as she awoke was the throb of her wrist. The next was the music drifting up from below, bringing with it the events that had taken place before she had lost consciousness.

She sat up abruptly making her head spin. Jessica raised a hand to her temple trying to massage away the headache while her mind cleared. After a minute, she slid from her bed where she'd been laid out. Crossing to the door, she gripped the handle. It refused to turn. She was locked in.

A wave of panic ran through her. She had to get out. She had to let people know that she would not marry Clifford Raker. They couldn't make her. Jessica froze. That was exactly what they planned. Clifford and her stepfather were going to force her to marry him. Her first instinct was to deny that it could happen, but she knew better.

She should've known something like this would happen. In just a month she would come of age and inherit Wellington Meadows. Bradley Calloway wouldn't let that happen, but would he marry her off to Clifford Raker? The answer was a resounding, yes!

He would take added pleasure in the fact that she despised the man. Raker was a crude abuser, with questionable honor. Raker and her stepfather had made the arrangement to steal her inheritance. Well, they may steal her inheritance, but they were not going to force her to marry him.

Heading across the room, she opened the armoire and stepped onto the shelf so she could reach the vase on top of it. Jessica pulled out the letter that had arrived a month before. Amos Isaacs had been their horse trainer her whole life until Bradley ran him off. The old man had helped raise her and was her best friend. He knew of her problems with her stepfather. He'd written when he had settled in California. She read again where he said he had put the land in her name too, just in case she ever needed to come, to get away from Calloway. Well, now she did.

Numbly, she sank to the bed as she thought about her mother. Tears burned Jessica's eyes. She couldn't leave her mother. Her mother needed her. Jessica paused when the truth hit her. Raker would not allow her access to anyone after the morrow. He would keep her locked away. She couldn't live like that. She couldn't stay, not even for her mother.

With tears still on her cheeks, she returned to the wardrobe, but this time she was calm and determined.

Jessica pushed aside the two beautiful party gowns that hung in there and pulled out her more practical everyday dresses. Setting them on the bed, she quickly gathered all necessities and the few items that were precious to her. Lastly, she added the jewelry which had belonged to her grandmother.

She paused looking down at the mountain of items, then turned back to the wardrobe. Taking out her favorite special gown, a light blue silk with ivory lace, she placed it on the pile then debated the large stack again. It was a lot to take, but since she might not be coming back, she decided it was what she wanted. And besides, she would be taking her horses so there wouldn't be any trouble carrying her belongings.

Jessica set aside one of her riding outfits then broke the pile into four smaller groups. She folded everything then wrapped them into the quilts that were from her trousseau. Once she got to the stable, she would wrap them in canvas before tying them to the pack saddles. She opened the window and realized the music no longer played. The moon was high in the sky attesting to the lateness of the hour.

Jessica peered out the window with the first bundle in hand, took a deep breath, and then let it drop. When no one came to investigate, she did the same with the other three. She let out a sigh of relief when the last one hit the ground.

She looked around for something for her to climb down on and then paused. First, she needed to change her clothes. The elegant gown with full slips might be perfect for a celebration, but not for climbing out a window and riding a horse.

She was just loosening the laces when she heard the scraping of the key in the lock. She stared frozen at the door. For an instant, Jessica debated jumping from the window but common sense prevailed, knowing she was apt to break something. Instead, she made a dash to close it. Jessica had only taken two steps from the window when whoever struggled with the lock finally got the key in and it opened.

Jessica gasped, drawing Clifford Raker's gaze directly to her. She never even considered it would have been him who opened the door, but his large frame filled the opening, blocking her escape as effectively as the door had.

Chapter Two

"So you're awake."

"What are you doing here?" She didn't try to sound civil.

"I came to make sure my new bride had recovered from her excitement." His words slurred out.

"I'm not your new bride, nor will I ever be."

"By noon tomorrow, you will be mine." His tone was harsh and threatening.

Jessica couldn't stop herself from taking a step back. He staggered slightly as he took several steps into the room, and she knew he was drunk. The look in his eyes also said he was dangerous.

When he looked from her to the bed Jessica felt sick. Then his eyes focused on the riding outfit there. Terror filled her.

"Planning to run out on me," he glared back at her. When Jessica refused to comment, he turned back to the door. She could hardly believe he was leaving. He wasn't.

Raker pushed the door closed and shoved the key into the lock. His burst of anger seemed to give him an unwelcome edge on the control of his drunken body.

"What are you doing?" She tried to keep her voice forceful and chastising, but fear made it crack. "Get out."

Her answer came with the punishing click of the lock. He turned to her.

"Such a fiery little thing. I've told you before how much I like that, but I'm afraid you'll have to be taught how to respect me. How to obey."

"I said get out." Her fear turned to panic as the man walked toward her.

"I think it's time to start the honeymoon."

"No!" She backed away feeling sick.

His lips tilted up in a cruel smile and he kept coming.

"I will not be touched until after my wedding." Jessica tried to draw on her courage, while edging around the room.

"I've waited long enough." He cut her off as she made a break for the window. "You think you can get away like last time, when your daddy saved you. He thought you were too good for me. You thought so, too. I should've had you."

"I was barely fifteen," Jessica objected as she shifted toward the other side of the room.

"But you were made for a man, just as you are now." His gaze ran over her again in leering anticipation.

"No!" She made a dash for the door. Even though it was locked, she tugged and pounded on it, yelling for help. Clifford's hand caught her hair yanking her back against his unyielding body, his other callused hand clamped over her mouth and nose, cutting off the cries and most of her air. The hand in her hair dropped to her stomach almost covering it entirely as he forced her tight to him.

Jessica tried to scream again, but the hand on her mouth tightened. Lights flashed in front of her eyes, her ears roared. The hand covering her mouth loosened.

"You're not going to faint again."

He gave her a harsh shake. "I want you awake for this. I want you to fight." He pressed his mouth close to her ear while he described what he would do to her.

The foul smell of his breath mixed with the fouler words, adding to her nausea. She tried to will herself to be sick and almost succeeded when she was shoved across the room, landing on the floor beside the bed. Before she could react, hands were on her again, lifting her up, dropping her on the bed. Clifford's larger body followed her smaller one down.

Immediately, Jessica began to push up and kick. She scratched and hit, but it made no difference to the harsh hands that groped at her body. The scream she got out ended with a numbing blow to her cheek.

Jessica clung to the pain to keep from slipping into the blackness which welcomed her. Unwilling to accept what was happening, she fought harder.

Raker easily knocked her flailing arms away. Her hand hit against the heavy lamp sitting on the nightstand. She latched onto it, but from the odd angle she was at, she couldn't lift it, but her struggling was enough to topple it over. The lamp struck squarely on the back of Raker's head with all its weight. A loud crack sounded a second before Raker went limp, crushing her even deeper into the mattress.

Lamp oil trickled through his hair and over his cheek. Jessica realized it was fortunate the lamp hadn't been lit, or she would have set them both on fire plus the bed and the house.

She shoved the thought aside and set out to do the same to the man. She tried to push the body away but it hardly moved. Tears filled her eyes. Determined, she pushed again finally getting him up enough to wiggle her way out.

Jessica stumbled back a few feet and wrapped her arms over her torn bodice and tried to keep from crying. There wasn't time for that, but as she looked at the bed, a wave of revulsion hit her body threatening to overwhelm her. She caught the sob then forced a breath into her constricting lungs. Now was not the time to fall apart. She had to get out of there.

Jessica took a minute and used several scarves to tie Raker to the bed, then she tied one across his mouth to gag him. She felt a wave of relief when she had him secured but didn't stop to relax. Moving behind the dressing screen, she changed into her riding clothes, leaving the torn ball gown where it fell.

She hesitated coming from behind the screen only a second before moving over to the still unconscious man. She checked his bonds over quickly then slid her fingers into his pocket to retrieve the key. Jessica snatched up the letter from Amos then unlocked the door.

She paused to check the hallway. Stepping out, she turned and relocked the door. She paused again outside her mother's room feeling a deep seeded longing but knew she couldn't risk taking the chance to talk to her.

Jessica crept down the stairs, fearful that at any moment someone would step around the corner and catch her. Her heart was pounding by the time she reached the bottom. Leaning against the wall, she put her hand over her heart to still it. She started for the door then paused again, turning back to the study.

As always, she felt comforted as she stepped into the room. It was her father's room. Bradley Calloway might have invaded the house, but he'd never been able to conquer the essence of her father here. In this room, as in the stables and fields, was how she would always remember her father.

Jessica felt calmer, sure of what she planned to do. By the moonlight coming through the window, she went to the gun case and took out the pistol that had been her father's. It was now hers. She fastened it around her waist. Even on the first notch, the belt hung low on her hips but it would stay on.

Next, she removed her father's saddle bags and loaded them with bullets for the pistol and her father's rifle. Then she took out his large hunting knife and the two smaller ones that he'd always carried. She almost missed the flint and steel he used to start fires but found it on her last look for what else she needed to take.

Jessica draped the bags over her shoulder. She almost felt like a thief sneaking out, but everything she took was hers. All Wellington Meadows had been left to her except the house, which was her mother's. Everything was to be kept in trust, managed by the executor until her eighteenth birthday or until marriage. The thought hit her with a certainty that that was why she was being forced into marriage. In one month she would have taken control of it all.

She pushed the thought out of her head to keep the terror of what almost happened from paralyzing her while she made it around the side of the house. The moon was almost full and lit the grounds, it would, therefore, be easier for her to be seen.

She found the bundles intact where she had dropped them. She knew she could carry only two at a time which meant two trips so she decided, instead of taking one load all the way to the stables, she would move them in steps to get her away from the house sooner.

Jessica picked up the first bundle and swung it over her back. It was difficult but she also managed to get hold of the smallest bundle. They were awkward but she made it away from the house, moving in relative silence, heading for some bushes that were a third of the way to the stables.

By the time she made it to the stables her arms ached from the loads. With relief, she lowered her burden. Slippers and Ruby were her only horses in the stable at the time. Her other horses were in the pasture, but they would come to her when she called.

She paused, wondering if she was foolish taking her horses, but her father had given them to her as birthday presents starting when she was eight. He, along with Amos, had helped her train them. She was not leaving them behind.

She wished she could take her father's stallion, Smokey, but he was too hard to handle around the fillies.

And it wasn't like she was leaving him totally behind. Two of her mares already carried his next generation. She had hoped to breed Lady to him soon. Well, things change. Once she got to California and found Amos, she could worry about horse breeding. For now, she just had to concentrate on getting away.

She decided to saddle Jasper because he could go the longest before she would need to switch him out. Jasper was her only gelding. He was Rosy's first foal. He was only three and had plenty of spirit, but he was a wonderful horse.

In the tack room, she found canvas to wrap around her bundles and also her father's bedroll. Though he hadn't used it often, he'd always kept it ready. Taking it and the other camp gear she fastened the bedroll on her saddle along with the rifle's scabbard, working quickly, aware of every minute she spent.

Jessica went out the stable side door to the pasture and made a soft clicking sound. By the time she made it the third time, the first of the large shapes moved toward her followed by several others. "That's my girls," she greeted the first two, rubbing their necks before leading the horses into the stable.

All her other horses were waiting for her when she came back out. She made sure each received a pat and praise. Jessica was almost tempted to take several of the other horses waiting but she knew it would be hard enough to handle what she already had.

Once all were loaded and ready to leave, she thought of food. Jessica debated a minute on going back to the house for it then decided against it. She had taken enough time and still had one more stop before she left the property.

A half mile away, down by the creek was her and her father's favorite spot and the hiding place for the money her grandmother had left her. The day that Bradley

Calloway moved into the house she had hidden the money there, nearly eight hundred dollars in gold coins.

Grandmother Wellington had been a feisty lady, who always said, 'A woman needed to be able to take care of herself.' She was certainly right, though Jessica figured her grandmother never would have envisioned this circumstance. Still, her grandmother was giving her the chance she needed to survive.

Jessica opened the stable doors and led the tethered horses out before swinging into Jasper's saddle. She took a last look back to the house where she'd been born and raised before leading the horses out on a walk so not to disturb anyone. It took only a few minutes to retrieve the money then she urged the horses into a gallop across the field to the road.

The ride gave her an opportunity to refine her plans. The first thing she needed to do was to reach Albert Hamilton, her father's executor. Mr. Hamilton lived an hour's ride away. She'd noticed he had not been at the night's gathering. Obviously, Bradley had failed to invite him. Mr. Hamilton would never accept the marriage plans without checking to see if it was her wish.

Jessica hated to wake him in the middle of the night but knew he would understand. She left the horses on the edge of his property and made her way to the back of the house. It took several knocks before she heard footsteps on the other side of the door.

"Who's there?" A male voice called out.

"Jessica Wellington, Mr. Hamilton."

"Jessica." She heard him exclaim as he fumbled to open the door. "What are you doing here at this time of night?" he asked, drawing her in. "What's wrong?"

Jessica felt tears begin to rise but brushed them away trying to compose herself.

"Is it your mother?"

She shook her head taking a deep breath. "Tonight we

had a party. Bradley announced that tomorrow I'd be marrying Clifford Raker at noon."

She didn't slow when the lawyer let out an exclamation. Now that she had started, it all came rushing out. She told about fainting and Raker coming to her room and her escape. Tears were streaming down her cheeks by the time she finished.

"Let me wake Martha to make you some tea." He patted her arm.

"Please, don't bother her."

"Nonsense, she would be upset if I didn't. Now sit and wait in my den. I will be right back."

Jessica sank into a chair too tense to relax. She was alert the moment he stepped back into the room.

"Now first thing," he began as he moved behind his desk to sit, "is to figure out how to stop them from forcing you into this marriage. Your father detested Raker. Trust me; I will do everything in my power to see that you are not forced into marrying him. Unfortunately, most people would see nothing wrong with the arranged marriage."

"I've already taken care of that. I'm leaving The Meadows. That's why I'm here. Is there any way I can leave you to continue to be the overseer of it, as you have been for my father? That way you could handle the hiring, oversee the running of the property and take care of an allowance for my mother. I know it's asking a lot."

The man waved the last comment away. "Of course it's possible, but where would you go?"

"To California. Amos sent me a letter. He knew how bad things were." She pulled out the letter and handed it to him, giving him a minute to read it.

"You cannot honestly be planning to go there."

"I am."

"That's wild country."

"I'll join a wagon train."

"Do you realize the distance we are talking about?"

"Other women do it."

"Yes, with their families, and a man to watch over them."

"I'm young and strong. I'm not like my mother. I can take care of myself."

"True. You're your father's daughter and a lot like your grandmother Wellington. That woman would have faced it on her own but still, I do not like it."

"But it is my choice."

The man nodded. "I could hire someone to accompany you."

"There's no time. If they find me, they'll force me to go back. I can't. I will not marry Clifford Raker."

"Yes, I understand that, but this is so drastic. I'd feel awful if something happened to you. It is such a wild and uncivilized area you are talking about crossing. I would be negligent if I did not try to talk you out of it."

"I understand, but that choice is made. You were a good friend to my father. He felt highly of you and he trusted you. That is why I'm asking you to remain executor of The Meadows. I don't want Calloway to be able to get his hands on it. Can it be done?"

The lawyer nodded. "I will need to make a length of contact time so he cannot just declare you dead without proof of a body."

"Can you make it cover for even if there is a body? That might stop him from killing me," she added and thought for a second that he was going to object to the possibility, but he nodded.

"It can be done. Shall we say five years from the last correspondence that way as you write, it can continue the length of time it is effective."

"Yes."

"Why don't you relax while I prepare it?"

"Please hurry and thank you."

This time the man waved her off to go to the kitchen to

his wife. By the time Martha Hamilton had fed her, he had the paper written and ready to sign.

Since there was no getting her to stay the night, Mrs. Hamilton forced a sack of food on her, before kissing her cheek by the door. Albert Hamilton, too, kissed her cheek. "Don't worry, I'll take care of everything and when Bradley comes looking, I won't say anything of where you're going but I will get someone to head him in the wrong direction; for a price." He winked, bringing the first smile to her lips since the night began.

"Thank you."

"I still dislike you traveling alone at night."

"I'll take care, but I must get started."

"I've heard in Springville there's a wagon train forming."

"I'll head there then. Even if they've left I might be able to catch them. Thank you again for everything."

"You're welcome. I wish you the best."

Once again Jessica fled into the night. Her adrenalin held her for several more hours. She managed to press on until almost dawn before she found herself falling asleep in the saddle. She led the horses off the road, hiding amongst a grove of trees. Jessica settled the animals then laid out her bedroll and dropped down on it in an exhausted sleep.

∽∾

Jessica pulled to a stop in front of the livery stable. When she stepped down from the horse after three days in the saddle, her legs were unsteady, the ground felt unfamiliar. She had awoken the first morning stiff and sore, and it had yet to leave her body as Jessica was determined to put as much distance behind her as possible.

A short burly man came out of the livery. "Can I help you?"

"Yes sir. I heard that there was a wagon train organizing here."

"Yes, miss. Swedish Hansen is the wagon master."

"Can you tell me where I might find him?"

"He's set his wagon up just down the street past the church. You married?"

Jessica jerked at the question. "No sir, but I'm of age."

"Well, I can tell you right now, if you're figurin' on going with them, they won't take a single woman."

Taken aback, Jessica wasn't quite sure what to say. "Ah, thank you but I'll go talk to him just the same. How much would it be to grain and rub down my horses?"

They agreed on a price and Jessica headed down the street. The walk felt good. She drew a few looks, many accompanied with smiles. The church was easy to find as were the wagons just past it.

A slightly plump woman was cutting vegetables at the tail gate while a large, balding man and a boy of about ten sat by a cold fire ring working on a harness.

"Mr. Hansen?" she greeted as he looked up.

"That'd be me," he said with a heavy accent and set down the harness to stand.

"My name is Jessica Wellington. I was wondering about joining your wagon train and when it was leaving."

"At first light, the morning after next. How many are there in your family?"

"It's just myself and horses. I'm not taking a wagon."

His features clouded. "You're not married?"

"No, sir."

"Not with your family?"

"No sir, I'm on my own. I'm going to my uncle in California." She decided it wasn't a complete lie because Amos had always been like an uncle to her.

"I'm sorry miss, but we can't have an unwed woman with us unaccompanied by her family."

"I don't understand."

"It's just not done."

"But I won't be any trouble. I can tend my own animals and take care of myself."

"It's not proper for a woman on her own. It causes too many complications and it's just not done," he repeated the ending.

"Please, I can pay my way."

"The offer is no good. The answer's still no. And I will tell you, no other wagon train will accept a lone, single woman."

"But I have to go."

"Then I would suggest you find yourself a husband. That should'na be hard. You're a pretty one, young and strong. You could probably find several men heading west that would be more than willing to marry you."

"I don't want a husband. I want to go west."

"Well, that will not happen without the other."

She knew she was not going to get anywhere with him. "Thank you anyway. Good day." She turned back toward town dejected.

"If you decide to find a husband, we leave at sunrise day after next," the wagon master called from behind.

Jessica acknowledged him but kept on walking. She knew she would not be there in the morning. She'd escaped one marriage. And, though any man was probably better than Clifford Raker, she wasn't in a hurry to look for one.

When she married, she wanted a man she could love and respect. Many might scoff at the foolishness, especially when she was always considered to be such a practical and serious young woman, not given to giggles and flirting. But that didn't mean she didn't want love over simple compatibility and servitude.

She also wanted to go west. She just had to figure out how. She was almost at the church when she passed a covered wagon that was being driven by a boy maybe fourteen or fifteen no bigger than her, but he handled the team with no problem. Beside him sat two girls about eight and three. Jessica smiled at the youngsters who gave her a little wave, but her attention darted back to the young man whose features were still that of a smooth-faced boy.

His lean body was hardly masked by the vest that would likely take at least another year or two for him to fill out. The shirt sleeves billowed out over arms that had yet to gain large more defined muscles. The wide brimmed hat covered not only his hair but shadowed most of his face. When he looked over and caught her staring at him, he tilted down his head covering more of his face, looking shyly away.

The action was well placed in Jessica's mind as she smiled and headed back to the livery. Pleased at the care that had been given to her horses, she was tempted to stay the night, but decided she could not risk the time. Besides, she had a plan to enact. She made it past the next town and another before she stopped at the edge of the following town, hidden back so no one would see her. She left the other horses, riding Misty into town.

The general store had all she was looking for. She tried to keep herself relaxed though she drew quite a bit of attention when she placed the boots, three pairs of pants, four shirts, a vest and coat, three pairs of leather gloves, two neckerchiefs and a wide brimmed hat on the counter.

"Is that everything, miss?" the store keeper asked skeptical.

"I think so." She added an accentuated sweet simplicity to her voice, deciding to play up the role she'd set for herself. "That's what my mama said. My brother is going out west. Mama wanted him set up right. I wish I could go too, but Abigail and Jacob are too young, and we're better off to let Joseph go first. Can you think of anything I might have missed?"

"Blanket, cooking utensils," he suggested.

"Oh, we have that. It was papa's and mama is well stocked on food supplies."

"You know, I don't recognize you from around here."

"Oh, we live over by Hampton," she mentioned the last

town that she had skirted. "Mama's upset with, oh, I guess I shouldn't say that. But anyway, she didn't want to get this there in town. You'll probably be seeing more of me as the summer goes on."

"I'm surprised she sent you and not your brother."

"He has some plowing to finish up before he leaves. I had to help this morning." As messy and tired as she felt, it probably looked like the truth. "Mama also wanted to surprise Joseph." She had almost forgotten the name she had used for her brother. "It's kind of for his birthday, though it's not until next month. Oh, mama said I could get two pieces of candy for each of us." She looked at the candy jars. "Let's see, may I have five of those and five whips.

"Is that it?"

She looked around the shop one more time. "Oh my, I almost forgot. Mama asked me to get her a new pair of sewing shears." Jessica went over and looked at them carefully before picking a pair. Then she added two spools of thread, a pack of needles and two dozen buttons. "That should be it."

The man added the items to his list and figured it. "That will be twenty-two dollars and fifteen cents." He looked at her. Jessica ran her eyes over the list. It was what she had figured and nodded.

Jessica took a small handkerchief from her pocket and untied it. She carefully removed the single twenty dollar gold piece and the two and half dollar piece she had placed there earlier and put them on the counter with an amount of apprehensiveness that she thought that the occasion might call for, but no way felt.

While the man tied her bundles with string, she asked. "Can you tell me a good place in town to eat? Mama said I could eat in town because I'll miss supper by the time I get home."

"The hotel across the street serves a good meal for a

fair price."

"Thank you."

"Take care, now," he said, handing her the change and the packages.

"I will. Good-bye." Jessica escaped outside letting out a big sigh. She never knew lying could be so exhausting, but she'd better get used to it. She was going to be living the biggest lie of all. With conviction, she headed for the hotel and a good, hot meal.

After retrieving her horses, she rode until nightfall before stopping. The minute Jessica laid down on her bedroll, she was asleep.

Raker had found her. The large man moved out of the shadows coming down on her before she had a chance to move. Harsh hands pulled at her hair. Jessica fought to get air in her lungs but couldn't seem to breathe for the heaviness on her chest. She tried to scream but nothing came out. She thrashed and struggled, but he was always after her, grabbing at her, pushing her down.

With a scream, she sat up. Sunlight cut through the leaves of the tree. The horses moved nervously where they were tethered a few feet away. The woods were quiet then the chatter of a squirrel cut the air.

Jessica brushed back her hair, which had come free during the night, and took a deep breath. The dream had come again. She reached up and brushed tears from her cheeks, vowing that this would be the last time she'd suffer tears because of Clifford Raker. After today, he'd never be able to find her.

With determination, she pushed back the blanket. She straightened her shoulders deciding not to let nervousness get a chance to settle in her stomach. She retrieved the scissors she'd bought the day before and a silver mirror that had been her grandmother's from her pack.

With the mirror braced on a couple of tree branches, she freed her waist length hair and ran a brush through it.

Jessica closed her eyes as she tried to steady her resolve. Picking up the scissors, she put them to the lock of hair just below her ear and cut it away, letting the long mahogany mass drop to the ground. She worked her way around the back until she could no longer see then she switched to the other side. Using her fingers to measure the length, she continued to work, ignoring the pool of hair around her feet.

Once she was satisfied it was as even as she was going to get it, she ran her fingers over her hair, which ended far too soon to feel normal. Self-consciously, she did it a couple more times, holding back the tears.

Funny how she had never given much thought to her hair. It was pretty hair, thick, a rich color that changed color as the light hit it. She had styled it as occasion demanded, but the only thing she was compulsive about her hair was to keep it clean, and that was just because she liked the way it felt, like fine silk. She bit her lip. It was still silky, just short.

Well, when she reached California, it could be grown again, and it really didn't look too bad, except maybe the front. She pulled a bit of hair over her forehead like she had seen the boys do, folding it up to see how it looked, making the decision she cut the bangs just above her eyebrows.

"Not bad," she said aloud to herself. She turned her head back and forth. She actually liked it. Her features were still feminine, but she wasn't finished with her disguise. First, she needed to wash the itchy mess. She headed to the small creek and realized this might be the last time she could wash with ease. For the next several months she would have to use caution.

The clothes were a little big, but that was all for the better. The old, man's money-belt that she had always used to keep her inheritance stashed in did a lot to mask her waist. She added a couple handkerchiefs as padding to add bulk and help keep the coins from making any noise. It felt heavy but it was also probably best to keep her money on her person at all times. She'd just have to get used to it. It wasn't any more uncomfortable than a corset.

Her bust was going to be a problem. Her chemise wouldn't be any help, although she could wear her corset over the money-belt which would smooth her down. She lifted the old corset she had been wearing and studied it a minute before removing the boning and laces. Opening it, she studied it again before she cut it in half lengthwise in half. She cut the ties in half then worked the laces back in.

Removing her shirt, she fitted the altered corset over her breasts and tightened it. The effect was perfect, as long as it stayed in place.

With the baggy shirt back on, she was sure no one would ever discern her shape but she added the vest to be certain. Jessica put the hat on her head and looked at herself in the mirror. The change was quite good.

Her face was a slight problem, but she had seen soft, 'pretty' faced boys before. She'd just have to be careful not to smile and to keep her head adverted. That would take some getting used to. She was used to meeting people straight on.

Bradley had said she was too sure of herself. He would have beaten it out of her but he hadn't dared when he found out Wellington Meadows was truly hers. She smiled wondering how he felt about what she'd done now.

In a more comfortable, happy mood, she grabbed something to eat, packed up, and was on her way. Jessica passed by the next town before trying out her disguise. Most people didn't pay much attention to her as a boy. She stayed only long enough to pick up a few supplies and be certain there were no wagon trains in the area before moving on.

Later that day, she tried another town with a bit more success. At the general store, she heard of a wagon train heading out of a town about thirty miles to the northwest. A surge of excitement rushed through her as she walked around gathering supplies, deciding it would draw less attention to herself if she didn't get them all in one place. She stopped at one more town that evening, picking up more supplies.

First thing the next morning, she added what she figured would be the last of what she needed. By the time she rode into Evansville, she had the packs on four of the horses filled to capacity. With her riding one horse, that left three she could rotate between.

Unlike the first wagon train she came to, she had no trouble finding this one on her own. Nine wagons already stood on the outskirts of town. People buzzed around them in preparation. There was an excitement in the air that was contagious, but it was tempered by a shot of nervousness. Jessica steadied herself and mentally went over her story one more time before approaching a woman working outside one of the wagons.

This was it. She took a deep steadying sigh.

"Pardon me," she kept her voice low. "Can you tell me who might be the wagon master and where I can find him?

The woman looked up briefly before returning to her work. "His name is Jacob Hammond. Try three wagons over there." She nodded her head to the side.

"Thank you, ma'am."

Jessica led her horses around the outside of the wagons in the direction indicated. Before she reached it, a barrel-chested man came out to greet her. He had a balding head and light blue eyes with wrinkles around them that spoke of a good nature. His tanned face and callused hands attested to hard work.

"Mr. Hammond?" Jessica ventured a guess.

"Yes, boy. You looking to sell some horses?" The man made a guess of his own. He looked the animals over, paying more attention to them than her.

"No, sir. I was wondering if I might be able to join

your wagon train."

His eyes came back to her, this time with more interest. Jessica tilted her head slightly forward, putting her face in shadow.

"You have a wagon coming with your family?"

"No, sir, there's just me and my horses."

"And you want to join a train?"

"Yes, sir."

"Even though the company has no oxen with the wagons, we'll be traveling slower than you could make it on your own."

"I'm aware of that, sir. But I have no one else to travel with and it would be foolhardy to try it alone."

"True enough. Where are you headed?"

"All the way to California. I have an uncle who went out last year."

"He knows you're coming?"

"Yes, sir."

"And your family?"

"My father died nearly two years ago. My mother remarried," she turned her head away. "He doesn't want me around. It was decided it was time for me to leave. The horses are mine for a new start."

The man looked from her to the horses and back. "It's a long way. It'll take us three months, barring any trouble."

"I'm prepared. I have my supplies all ready, and I can care for myself and my horses. I won't be any trouble."

The man was quiet a minute then nodded. "Well, we're all taking the California trail. I guess we can always use another man, even if he's still only half grown. You'll have to pull your weight and you'll be expected to help out."

"Yes sir."

"How old are you boy?"

"Fifteen."

The man nodded again. "All right, you can come along."

"Thank you, sir."

"Name's Jacob, and your's?"

Jessica swallowed, "Jess Wells."

"All right, Jess. We leave at first light. If there is anything you'll be needin', I suggest you get it this evening. We won't wait."

"I'll be ready."

"I'll send my son over with a list to make sure you've got everything. You can camp anywhere here that there's a space."

Jessica waited until she'd led the horses out of ear shot before she released the breath she'd been holding. She'd made it. She was accepted on a wagon train. She was really headed west.

Chapter Three

"You don't have a wagon?" The young boy came up behind Jessica just as she began to remove the packs. He was about six years old, with dark brown hair and eyes.

"No, I don't," she answered casually before continuing with what she was doing. "What's your name?"

"Jon Hammond."

"Nice to meet you." She held out her hand. "I'm Jess Wells."

The boy shook hands. "I was to bring you this." He held out a paper. "I was also to make sure you could read. If not, Papa said he'd come and help you."

"I can read."

"Are those your horses?"

"Yes."

"Do they have names?"

"Yes, this is Lady and this is Willow, that's Slippers, Rosy, Ruby, Misty, Midnight Star, but I just call her Star, Domino and Jasper."

"Star because she's black and has a white star on her head."

"Yes, her mother was completely black. She got the star from her father."

"She's beautiful."

"Yes, she is. She's six years old and likes to run."

"I'm six years old and like to run."

Jessica found herself smiling. "I could guess you do."

"We're going a long ways."

"Yes."

The conversation was interrupted by a deep male voice. "Those are some good looking horses. How much you asking for them?"

Jessica forgot what she was going to say as she turned to the man she hadn't heard approach, which was surprising given he was over a full head taller than her, putting him well to six foot. He had wide shoulders and thick dark hair that was nicely trimmed. His strong jaw was clean shaven with a deep cleft in it. His nose was slightly crooked as if it had been broken at one time. But it was his eyes that caught her. They were as blue as if they had been pulled from the sky.

Jessica jerked out of her study of him as a look of confusion passed over his face. She dipped her head slightly to let the brim of the hat shade her face. "They're not for sale."

"Pardon me, I saw you talking to the wagon master and presumed. Good day."

The man started to turn away when Jon spoke up in an excited voice. "Mr. Hawke. This is Jess. Jess is going with us."

"Is that right?" The man turned back and looked her over again. "Are your parents still coming?"

"I'm on my own."

"Oh, not bringing a wagon?" It was more of a statement than a question but Jessica answered it anyway.

"The horses can carry all my needs and belongings."

He nodded. "That's a nice string of horses."

"My father was breeding them."

"No stallion?"

"My father was riding him when he had his accident." That much was true, and the man took the answer as she had intended with another nod.

"I have a nice stallion you might want to take a look at. Though, I figure we'll have a time watching him on the trail to keep him away from your mares."

"Ruby and Slippers have already been covered. I hadn't been planning on going west at the time."

"How much longer?"

"Ruby has six to seven weeks. Slippers about a week after. I don't plan to have either of them carrying anything and this is the second colt for both. They did well the first time."

"Then you shouldn't have any trouble. The wagons will be moving slow enough but holler if you need help."

"Thank you, Mr. Hawke."

"Nathan." He stuck out his hand.

"Jess," Jessica didn't hesitate to shake it, but her throat went dry when her gloved hand was enveloped by his. It was only held for a couple shakes but her hand felt foreign when he released it.

"Well, I imagine you have much to prepare."

"Yes."

"Jon, you want to walk back with me?" the man asked.

"Yes, sir. Goodbye, Jess."

"Goodbye Jon."

Jessica watched the man and the boy walk away. The boy's open acceptance and friendliness was nice but made her nervous. She would have to be careful around Jon. It would be easy to forget her role of pretending to be a boy.

She wouldn't have to worry about that around Nathan Hawke. Her heart took time to return to a normal beat. He was a disconcerting man; tall and rugged beneath his clean-cut appearance. He looked like he belonged out it the wilds of the frontier. She would have to say he was handsome. Though, she knew much better looking men, none had ever disturbed her as much. Then again, he would be married which didn't matter to her, but she decided she would just have to stay away from him.

೦೩೮೦

Jessica looked up at the clear starry sky and sighed in relief. During the first several days they passed a number of scattered towns. But after seven days on the trail, civilization had fallen behind. The stiffness that she'd felt from the long days in the saddle had ended before she had met up with the wagon train, so now her only difficulty was trying to keep her distance from the others to keep her secret.

She had gotten used to not looking directly up at people so they couldn't get a good look at her face. She also didn't speak much and limited her replies to one word or short answers. She knew she had developed a reputation as a loner or that maybe she was a little odd. She didn't really like it, but it suited her needs well.

Jessica made sure she did extra service for others, like gathering firewood or helping tend other horses once hers were done. Tonight she was on watch. Four men were assigned each night. This was her first time, and she had drawn the second watch.

The night was crisp and clear. The bugs kept up a constant chatter joined in by a few other nocturnal animals. Jessica found herself jumping now and then at the sounds, though the night was peaceful. She in fact, found the evening beautiful. Catching herself yawning, she pulled herself up to take another walk around the camp.

She heard a child making a fuss in one of the wagons and continued on. The moon was bright enough for her to pull out her father's pocket watch and check the time. It was almost time to wake her relief, Nathan Hawke.

The man still disturbed her. More since she learned he was single, a widower to be exact. Which she found terribly sad for him to be alone at twenty-four; he seemed to be a good man. She had watched him help out other people, and take time to bend his six foot plus frame down to talk to a child on their own level. He was also acting as one of the train's scouts.

A twig snapping startling her. Jessica froze, listening. The sound of footsteps was barely audible over the beating of her heart. Pulling back into the shadows, she watched and listened.

Her heart jumped in fear when she saw the shadow of a man pass one of the wagons heading toward her. Jessica carefully slid her pistol free, working her hand on the grip, making it feel more comfortable. With a steadying breath, she leveled the gun in the man's direction and followed his progression as he moved closer.

"Jess." Her name was said in a low husky voice she immediately recognized, though in the last week she'd avoided him. In the time it took her to react, he repeated her name.

She swallowed back the lump that had risen in her throat and stepped out of the shadows. The man jerked slightly but she had an impression that he knew she was there.

"There you are boy." It almost seemed that Hawke stressed the 'boy'. "Is all well?"

"Yes," Jessica kept her answer to one word.

"I'm your relief so you can turn in now."

She nodded starting to move past. He shifted slightly and she wondered if he might try to stop her as she hurried toward where she had her bedroll laid out a ways from the others.

CR80

Nathan watched the young man hurry away. As always, the lad seemed to be nervous and jumpy. Then again, he guessed it must be hard for him being alone at the age of just crossing into manhood.

Maybe that was where his own odd feelings were coming from. He felt unsettled around the young man. He found himself looking out for Jess, though the boy didn't seem to need much help. And even more so, unwilling to ask or receive it.

Maybe Jess had to prove that he could take care of himself. Well, as long as Jess was doing well he would let the boy be. It was good for the youth's self-confidence. He would just keep an eye out to make sure things were done and Jess was safe.

Nathan wondered again why he was making himself the young man's guardian. Jess was of age to have his own belongings and make his own way. Jess really didn't need him, and he had his own wagon, stock, plus the wagon train to worry about since he agreed to act as one of the scouts. But there was one main reason he watched over Jess, there was no one else to do it.

ᏣᎬᏃᎠ

Jessica was a little nervous riding Jasper through the woods. It wasn't that she minded being in the forest by herself or even feared getting lost and unable to find the wagons again. She wasn't even bothered by hunting. She had gone with her father quite often.

No, Jessica's fears were still locked on being found out. She never imagined it would be this hard deceiving the members of the wagon train day after day. Everyone had been so wonderful to her, accepting even though she stayed aloof.

She tried to be helpful but still apart. A smile etched its way across her lips. Young Jon Hammond had been the only one who was difficult to avoid. Quite often, she would turn around to find him following her or watching, waiting for her to talk to him. Jessica couldn't make herself ignore the boy. He was so cute.

Nathan Hawke seemed to also be watching her, but unlike Jon, she didn't find him comfortable. The uneasiness she felt around him had not dissipated at all in the last three and a half weeks.

The deer leapt from the woods startling her almost to the point of losing her seat as Jasper shied. "No," Jessica exclaimed aloud as the deer bounded away. She should have been paying more attention to what she was doing. The wagon train needed the fresh meat the buck would have provided.

For the last two weeks, every other day, three or four of the men were sent out for game to be divided among the wagons. This was her first time on the hunt, and now because of her thoughtlessness, she'd let the opportunity for a large amount of meat slip by. What made her feel even worse is she had not heard a single shot as yet, so no one else had been successful.

Had the buck gone far? She urged Jasper in the direction it had bounded.

A short ways ahead the trees opened into a meadow. There in the center stood the buck, totally unconcerned about her presence. He was almost too beautiful to shoot, but a steady supply of meat was important.

In slow motion, she raised her gun and sighted in on the animal. Her finger tightened on the trigger, pulling back. The butt of the gun slammed into her shoulder. The shot echoed over the meadow. For a second, as the deer stood there, she thought that she had missed, and then just as she was prepared to fire again, it dropped to the ground. Gun ready, she rode forward but the animal stayed down. As she drew nearer she could see it was dead.

Putting the gun back in its scabbard, she swung down. Jessica wasn't sure if the tears that rose in her eyes were for the beautiful buck or with her frustration of not knowing for sure what she was to do now or how she was going to do it. Taking a deep breath, she pulled the knife from her belt. One step at a time. Though she had never cleaned an animal by herself before, she had watched her father do it.

When it took all her strength to roll the deer over, she realized there was no way she was ever going to be able to get it on Jasper's back.

"Need a hand?"

Jessica spun hearing the man's voice behind her.

"Sorry, I didn't know you didn't hear me come up," Nathan Hawke said as he dismounted in an easy motion.

"I was trying to figure out how to get it back to the wagons."

"Yes, considering it probably weighs twice what you do." He smiled, pulling his knife. "Nice shot. I was just through the trees when I heard it. He ought to supply enough meat for a couple days." The man knelt down making swift work of cleaning the animal, directing her without commenting on her awkwardness.

"Do you want me to put it on Titan or up on your horse?"

"It doesn't matter. Jasper will carry it."

Going to his horse he untied a roll of sack cloth. "This will protect your saddle and gear."

"Thank you, I hadn't thought about that," she said, helping him wrap the deer.

"Didn't you ever go hunting with your father?" he probed and Jessica guessed it was because she obviously didn't know what to do.

"I did hunt with my father but usually someone else took care of the kill," she mumbled.

"You must have come from a large farm."

"Yes."

"Why did you decide to leave?"

She hesitated a moment then the words seemed to come on their own. "My father died a year and a half ago. Things changed."

"What of your mother. Did she not need your help?" Nathan kept pressing. This was the most he'd gotten out of the young man who tended to close up around people.

"She remarried." The boy's head lowered farther down.

"You were not welcomed by her new husband," he said in understanding. It probably added to the boy's self-doubt.

"He made life difficult."

"So you left."

"There was no other choice."

"You took the horses," he stated.

The youth's head snapped up, a glare lit Jess' face with fire. "They're mine. I received one each year for my birthday."

"Whoa, I'm sorry," Nathan cut him off. "I wasn't insinuating that you stole them. I apologize."

"I apologize also." The head went back down so the hat brim once more hid his face. "I was not happy about leaving as I did, but as I said, there was no choice."

"It must've been difficult."

"It was." Jessica paused for a moment to keep the tears from rising. She was not going to cry in front of Nathan Hawke. She'd worked too hard to convince everyone she was a boy to lose it crying over something that was in the past. Besides, she was better off out of her stepfather's control and Clifford Riker's reach.

"We better get the deer loaded and back to the wagons."

Jessica knew she wasn't much help getting the deer on Jasper, but it didn't take long to realize Nathan didn't need much help. She figured her assistance was to boost her, a young man's ego, rather than need.

"This is a good size animal. There isn't going to be much room for you on the horse. Why don't you ride with me and we can lead your horse?"

"Jasper doesn't like to be led." As soon as the words were out of her mouth, Jessica knew her objection wouldn't work. She had led Jasper; along with the other horses; numerous times in the past weeks.

"We should be able to manage. Cinch tight the tie strap." He moved to his horse and swung fluidly into the saddle and stretched out a hand for her, kicking his foot out of the stirrup.

Jessica hesitated. She had never ridden a horse with a man other than her father and Amos. That would put him in a far too intimate contact with her, but there seemed to be no way to object. He didn't know she was a woman. Reaching out she gripped his hand, raising her foot to the stirrup.

For a moment, Jessica almost got the feeling that he was going to lose hold of her. She started to fall back. Then, he looked down at their hands and he pulled her up on the horse. She swung her leg over and settled behind him, keeping as much space as possible between their bodies.

"Sorry about that," Nathan said, unsure how to explain he almost dropped him because the boy's hand felt startling feminine in his hand. He wasn't sure if it was the small size in the leather gloves that made it seem so, but it bothered him. As did the heat from the boy's body. Though the boy kept rigidly away from him, heat radiated through, raising a totally inappropriate reaction, a reaction that was becoming familiar around Jess.

Biting back a curse, he tried to shove his thoughts away. He had heard of men that preferred men, but the notion was sickening to him. He should've taken a wife before leaving. Widow Larsen had shown her interest as had the Davis girl, but the Davis girl was only fifteen and that would have been indecent since he would be almost ten years her senior. Then again it was not nearly as indecent as being disturbed by a fifteen year old boy-man. Then again his feelings around Jess were not sexual. They were just disturbing, like being outside in a violent storm.

"Where are you going to end your journey?" Nathan decided to break the quiet with a question. "Are you going on to Oregon or south to California?"

"California. I have an uncle who's there. He claimed some land in both our names. He sent me a map of how to get there."

"That's fortunate. How long has he been there?"

"He left just over a year ago. He was my father's horse

trainer. When my mother remarried, my stepfather forced him out."

"So he knew of your problems with your stepfather?"

"Yes, that's why he sent the letter. He was always like a second father to me. He told me about the land. There is almost no snow in winter except for in the mountains. The valley is lush and green. He said it would be excellent for raising horses and anything else. He is already working on a room for me on his cabin."

"That sounds good. He knows you're bringing your horses then?"

"He knows I would never leave them. Jasper is one of the last horses he trained."

"He did a good job."

"Yes, he is excellent, but he's getting old. He should have remained at our farm for the rest of his life, not having to cross the wilds to settle a new home."

"Do you think he minded?" Nathan asked.

"No." It didn't take much thought before the answer came out. "He would've enjoyed the challenge. He's not a person to sit around. And he really doesn't like to be told he can't do something."

"And what about you, are you like that?"

"Amos said I'm like a spirited fi … horse." She caught her slip.

"Hard to handle and go where you please."

"Yes, he always said I was hard headed, but my father said that spirited horses were the best to have."

"He must have been a patient man."

"He was. I used to love watching him work with a new horse. He'd talk to them and they'd listen."

The man in front of her nodded.

Jessica realized how silly that sounded, but he accepted it because many times she had seen him do the same. Just the day before they were fording a river and one of the wagons had bogged down, and when the horses balked, it was Nathan Hawke who had entered the river.

He caught the harness and talked to the horses until they settled and worked together. They freed the wagon and he was able to lead them out.

"You do the same."

This time the man in front of her didn't answer.

"It's a gift you know." She couldn't seem to remain silent. "A talent and it's rare."

Nathan didn't know what to think of the words the boy had said, but he couldn't help but feel pleased. The respect in the tone warmed him. His affinity with horses had always been dear to him, but he knew most people never saw it. His wife never had. She had always pushed him toward business though it really held no interest to him. For years he had tried and had been successful in giving her a large home, and all the latest fashion she could desire, but when she had died, he no longer cared to live a life that didn't fit him.

"I enjoy working with horses," he said simply. He was relieved when the boy behind him remained silent. The young man was too disturbing for him.

They were welcomed with joyful greetings when they approached the wagons. The news of the kill quickly sped up the line that there would be fresh meat for all for supper that night.

Nathan headed directly for his wagon which was being driven by young Joseph Hammond. Jess' horses were tied to the back of the Hammond wagon at the lead.

"I'll get off here," Jess said just before he slid off the horse once again leaving Nathan shocked. "I'd like to check on my other horses. Is it all right if I leave Jasper with you?"

"That would be fine," Nathan said talking down at the hat brim. He wondered if he'd ever talk to the boy face to face. Jess really needed to get over his shyness. "We still have a good ways to go before we make camp. I'll take care of the deer, then return him to you."

"I'd appreciate it." The voice came as the boy stepped back, rubbing his gloved hand over the blaze on the horse's nose before he turned to go.

Nathan shook his head then turned his attention to Joseph engaging the thirteen year old into a conversation, thinking Joseph was nearly as big as Jess. Joseph was going to be big like his father. Nathan had no way of knowing what Jess' father was like, but he figured that Jess wouldn't be a very large man. Still, he could do a lot of growing. He might be late in getting his growth.

He hoped for the boy's sake it wouldn't be long until he started to mature. With his size, and the soprano voice, though he tried to keep it low, if you put Jess in a dress and added some padding, he could pass for a girl.

Chapter Four

The fires crackled and conversations hummed over the meadow. Jessica let out a contented sigh and checked on the brisket she had in the Dutch oven. Dinner wouldn't be long now. After that, she could sneak down to the stream to bathe.

Her biggest challenge was cleanliness which had always been one of her priorities. She sighed again. She might wear smudges on her cheeks at times to help with her disguise, but she didn't have to be dirty underneath.

The sound of someone coming out of the trees startled her out of her reverie. Jess turned to watch Nathan walk from the trees carrying his hat in his hand. The evening sun made the drops of water glisten in his hair, making it darker than normal. He looked clean but weary. Jessica glanced to where his wagon waited. The horses were unhitched and tended, but no fire was going and nothing else was set up.

She had seen him cutting up the deer and seeing that everyone got a portion, and then he went to help Mr. Fields, who had a problem with one of his team. He always helped others. She respected that. Looking at his unprepared camp, she felt a wave of empathy for him though she knew someone would offer him a meal. She looked back again seeing the tiredness in him.

"Mr. Hawke, would you like something to eat? I have plenty." She wasn't sure who was more surprised by the invitation when she realized the words had come out of her mouth.

He nodded and came toward her. "I appreciate it." He

settled by the fire with a groan. "It's been a long day. I was on late guard duty last night. It made for an early morning. Bed will feel good tonight."

Jessica moved the Dutch oven off the coals and started serving up the food.

Nathan looked pleased at the large amount of food she piled on the plate. "I was near dreading the thought of having to prepare myself dinner tonight," the man kept talking. "In fact, I was almost resigned to the fact of just going to sleep without."

"That's not good." Jessica again spoke without thinking. "A man needs a good meal."

"My mama used to say nearly the same thing. I suspect it's true." He accepted the plate. "Smells good. You handle the cooking better than I do."

"I try." She felt her cheeks warm and tilted her face away. She glanced over when she heard the sound of pleasure.

"You're a good cook, boy."

"My father thought it was important that I spend time in the kitchen though it wouldn't likely be needed of me. And Ruth, our cook, was pleasant to be around. She let me know I was never in the way, even when I made a mess."

"We both owe your Ruth our thanks." He was thoughtful for a minute before continuing. "It must have been a large place that you grew up on, if you had a cook and all. I'm still surprised you'd leave it. Shouldn't it have gone to you?"

Jessica hadn't even realized how much she had revealed until he questioned her. "It was a large farm, mainly we raised horses. The best horses you've ever seen." She knew she sounded like a bragging boy but it was the truth. "I actually do retain ownership of what was left to me. My father's executor will oversee its running for me until I make a decision on what to do with it."

"Want to see if you can make it on your own first?"

"Yes," she said simply because it was the easiest answer.

"Well, I agree you have some fine looking horses. Your two expecting mares seem to be doing well."

She nodded. "They're doing fine. I'm figuring the middle of next week for the first foal." She was silent a moment before she continued while she added another stick to the fire. "You were right about the pace of the wagons. Even if I have to wait up a whole day, I will have no problems catching up."

With his mouth full, Nathan nodded his agreement then swallowed. "Let me know if you need a hand. By the way, you have a mare that is drawing attention from Titan."

"That would be Lady. She's never been bred before. I'll try to keep an eye on her." A wave of embarrassment ran over her.

"That might not be enough," he commented dryly.

Jessica nodded letting her mind drift. If she would've remained at home she would've bred Lady this season with her father's stallion. She wished again she could have brought him, but he would have been too hard to handle. And after all she had Domino who was a yearling but already showing the strength and excellence of his sire. So there was a future there.

Hawke continued eating his excellent meal as the boy fell silent, lost in his thoughts. He wondered about asking Jess if he would be interested in sharing chores. It wasn't the first time he'd thought of it, but Jess always seemed to want to be on his own. Then there was the disturbing awareness that came over him when he was near the boy. It almost reminded him of his stallion sniffing the air around Lady.

Now that was a disturbing thought. A shiver ran though him. He'd been up far too long. He shook it off and shifted back to the horses.

Nathan figured there was no way to keep the horses

apart. Titan already had her scent and was just waiting for the right time which Nathan figured was drawing near.

He scraped what was left on the plate into one last bit, savoring the taste a minute before he spoke. "Well, thank you for the meal, I appreciate it. I'll say good night. I'm worn out." He stood and stretched his arms over his head, then reached down for his plate and placed it in the wash pan.

"Night, Mr. Hawke."

"I thought we got past the mister. It's Nathan or just Hawke. No need for airs out here."

The boy paused then nodded.

❦

Jessica watched the man walk into the night. She had been trying not to think of him as Nathan or Hawke. That was just too intimate and there was also something that was just too disturbing to her senses about him.

❦

The morning started off with heavy clouds. It wasn't the first storm they'd faced, there had been several rainy days being the season for it but as the day progressed, so did the feel of the storm. It thickened the air and the sky began to darken ominously.

The wagons pushed hard, stretching to reach the river ahead of the rain. The original plan was to camp on this side and wait to ford in the morning when the horses were fresh, but the storm changed that. If it was as bad as feared it could swell the river, adding danger or even holding up the crossing.

They finally reached the bank late in the afternoon, fortunately they found the crossing in good condition from the wagon train in front of them. With only a brief rest the first wagon was led into the river.

Half the wagons were across when the first sprinkles of rain began to fall. There were still three left when the first lightning strikes flickered in the distance. Jess handed little

Emmy to her mother inside the wagon and turned to watch the crossing wagon crest the bank, one more down.

Rivers were tricky, anything could happen, and storms made it more dangerous. Her job was to ferry women and children across. It was safer than having them in the wagons in case of trouble.

Jasper blew out a deep breath of air and Jessica leaned forward, stroking a gloved hand down over his neck. He didn't like the storm. "Easy boy," she murmured, feeling his muscles quiver.

Even from where she sat, she could see the muscles tighten on the pulling team trying to find footing on the slippery river bottom. The wagon moved forward with constant encouragement from the driver. They were nearing the slope out of the river when lightning spilt the sky followed immediately by a clap of thunder.

The shrill cry of the pulling team echoed. The team tried to bolt in fear. One of the large horses almost went down as it slipped. Jessica felt her breath catch as a rider moved in next to the panicked animals.

Water swirled around them. Nathan Hawke talked to the beasts, calming them, then after a moment, Nathan motioned for Mr. Richmond to urge them forward. The horses dug their hooves into the muddy bottom. They strained together and the wagon pulled forward, free of the muck. As soon as the team lunged up the bank, Nathan turned back to the last wagon, his wagon.

He rode over, stopping long enough in front of the team to say something to each horse and reached a hand over to rub behind the closest Belgium's ear. He stepped from his horse to the wagon box and took the reins from Jon Hammond's hands, then lifted the boy to Titan's back.

Nathan had the best team, but even they were nervous with the lightning crackling in the distance and moving closer. It could be a very tricky crossing. Most of the attention was focused on the wagon, but Jess forced hers away and urged Jasper into the water heading for Jon.

"Come on Jon," she said closing in on the boy.

"Mr. Hawke's letting me ride Titan all by myself because I did such a good job holding the team."

"You did do a good job." Jessica knew he had just held the reins with the brake set and that Nathan's horses wouldn't have moved until commanded, but the boy beamed. "How about we try to beat Mr. Hawke to the other side? We're going to have to hurry to get wood and a fire going so we can warm something to eat before the rain gets harder."

"Papa thinks we're in for a bad'n."

As the boy rode toward her, Jessica resisted the urge to reach for the stallion's reins. Titan was pretty good mannered for a stallion, but Jessica still angled Jasper next to him.

"I think he's right. You did a very good job with the wagon."

The boy nodded and sat up tall.

The rain turned into a downpour just after dinner. Everyone climbed into their wagons to sleep, instead of sleeping under them or just under the stars.

Jessica had first watch and by the time it was finished, she was miserable. Her slicker kept most of the rain off, but was she still soaked through and she hadn't had time to fashion a shelter between tending her horses and her watch.

She figured she'd just throw her bedroll on a canvas, under one of the wagons. That is what she had done on the other occasions that it rained, though none had been a downpour like tonight. It wasn't like she had much choice. It was one of the disadvantages of not having a wagon, along with having to load and unload the horses every day.

Jessica moved closer to the remaining fire that she had managed to keep going and pulled out her father's pocket watch, angling it to catch the light. Thankfully it was time to wake her relief.

She made her way to Mr. Hayes's wagon. "Mr. Hayes," she said softly trying to wake the man but not disturb others that might be close. She waited. When she got no answer, she tried again. "Mr. Hayes it's time for your watch." Again there was no answer. Jess wasn't sure what to do next. She definitely didn't want to push back the opening to wake the man.

Emery Hayes was her least favorite man on the train. Like Nathan, he was a widower with no children, but unlike Nathan, he was a gruff, lazy man, who wasn't overly clean. Most of all, she didn't like how he treated his horses. It wasn't that he was actually cruel. He just didn't treat them very well in her opinion.

"Mr. Hayes." She raised her voice hoping she didn't wake up those in the next wagon. She was wet, cold and wanted to at least get some sleep tonight, though the storm made it unlikely. "Mr. Hayes." Finally her anger rose enough that she reached out and pulled away the opening. "Mr. Hayes," she said sternly, while still trying to keep her voice low.

There was a grunting sound then a grumble. "Go away boy." The words were slurred out.

"It's time for your watch."

"I said go away, ya welp." The man shifted and ignored her.

That was it, her anger blew. She reached in to shake the man. "Get up, you have watch."

"Aye, you're letting water in." The deep voice grumbled angrily.

"Get up," she stressed her words.

"Get!"

Jess didn't see the hand coming from in the darken wagon. It struck in a glancing blow that caught her more on the arm than her shoulder, but it sent her sliding in the mud. She was going down. At the last minute, a hand clamped around her arm stopping her fall then righted her.

"What's going on here?" Nathan Hawke growled not looking at her but into the wagon. "Hayes, aren't you to be on watch?"

"Ain't well." A grumble came from within.

"Well enough to hit Wells."

"Didn't hit the boy, he's letting water in my wagon. I got ta sleep 'ere."

"I'm sure Wells would like to get some sleep, too. Now out."

There was a curse and more grumbling, but Jessica could hear movements within the wagon.

Nathan turned back to her. "I put your bed roll in my wagon. There's no place dry to lay it out here," he added as if cutting off her argument.

"But," Jessica looked at him from under the brim of her hat.

He continued. "Why don't you go get in it, I'll see to Hayes."

"I can't take your wagon," she objected. The thought of not sleeping on the ground sounded heavenly, but she couldn't sleep next to Nathan Hawke or any other man. Just the notion made her heart race. He might think her a boy, but she knew different. It would be indecent. She couldn't do it.

"You can't sleep out here, and there is no other place except Hayes' wagon. I can't see him volunteering it or for that matter you accepting."

"I'd rather take ill then sleep there." Tired, Jessica answered without thinking.

"Then it's settled, go on." He motioned her away but before Jessica could move Hayes stumbled from his wagon, falling back, landing on her, nearly taking her down. Again Hawke caught her, this time pulling her out of the way. All his attention was fixed on Hayes. "You've been drinking," Nathan growled low in a voice.

"Just enough to fight off the weather." The man's

words were slurred and he wobbled.

Jessica realized there was no doubt, he was drunk.

It was obvious that Nathan knew also. "You …" Nathan paused fighting back his anger, "know the rules. Go back to bed. You're in no condition to be on watch. But this isn't finished. Tomorrow there will be a council."

Hayes cursed. "I can watch."

"I'm not risking it," Nathan countered leaving no doubt the decision was final.

Hayes glared at Jessica for a moment, cursed again, then lumbered back into his wagon.

Nathan turned back to her. "Go to my wagon Jess."

"You're taking his watch." She knew the answer before she said it.

"No choice."

"It was to be your night off," she objected. Not that it would change a thing.

"Yeah, well I'm already out here and wet. I might as well stay."

For a moment she couldn't take her eyes off the man. It was so dark she could hardly see him. Not that she needed to, his image was engraved in her mind. An uncomfortable feeling settled in her, almost like she was having trouble breathing. She gave herself a mental shake, pushing the thoughts from her mind. She nodded and turned away.

CB&O

Hawke watched the young man walk away, noticing his stride was off. He couldn't quite put a finger on it, but it was different. Jess Wells was different all around. He just couldn't quite figure the boy out. Jess' shyness bothered him, but it was more.

He wished he could get Jess to look at him. He was getting tired of looking at the ever present hat brim. It wasn't unusual for him at his height, he looked down on a lot of men, but they usually tilted their heads up. But not

Jess. If anything, he tilted his further down, unless it was night, then he seemed to have no problem meeting him or anyone else straight on.

Chapter Five

It was a mistake, Jessica thought lying on the soft down mattress over the bottom of the wagon. Nathan's smell curled around her. A masculine smell that always seemed to cling to him, but it wasn't unpleasant. Not like many men of her acquaintance. She sighed. It felt so good to be dry, comfortable, and to feel protected. With another sigh she slipped into sleep.

Two hours later when Nathan crawled into the wagon the figure in the bedroll didn't even move. Jess' breathing was still and even. Quiet as possible Nathan shucked his wet clothing and settled into the bed he'd left. It took only a couple minutes for the blankets to start warming his body.

He was tired but sleep didn't want to come. He was aware of the body next to him. He shouldn't have put Jess' bedroll in here and insisted the boy stay, but he couldn't leave him to sleep in the mud either when there was room here. If the boy just didn't disturb him so.

Nathan was afraid he was becoming a sick man. Every once in a while he would, look at Jess and think he was looking at a woman. He could almost picture him in a dress, but in his mind Jess'd have womanly curves, curves that would interest a man.

That was it, he was getting sick. Ready to be locked away. He cursed under his breath. He should have married before heading out west.

ᏣᏴ

Nathan didn't want to surface from the realm of sleep. He didn't want to let go of the woman's soft body pressed up against him. It had been too long since he'd known that kind of pleasure. He drew in a deep breath. It was a gentle fragrance to his senses.

Outside he heard the clattering of people moving. The wagon train, his mind focused on reality, still reality didn't want to focus, looking to the person that during the night had pressed to his side.

The features were beautiful, the skin soft and smooth looking, even under the layer of dirt. Lashes were long and dark. Lips full, bow curved. Jess a beautiful – '*boy*'. The word yelled in his mind and Hawke scrambled up and away.

Jess jerked up, dazed, his eyes widened.

"Time to get moving," Nathan growled, turning away, pulling on his clothes and boots.

It was morning. Horrified, Jessica scrambled up. She had been sleeping next to a man. Too tired, she hadn't occurred to her that after his watch he would be coming back here to sleep. It had been so foolish of her. What would happen if he found out she was a woman. She shuddered, not willing to think about it.

She had to get going. There was work to do. It sounded as if the rain had stopped, but it was going to be a rough day with the mud left from the night.

Jessica still had her shirt and trousers on, but she was glad Nathan Hawke was already gone. She pulled on her vest and coat. After putting on her hat, she made quick work of rolling up the bedroll. Then, with her feet hanging over the back of the wagon, she pulled on her boots, before jumping down. Luckily the sky was clear, and luckier, Nathan Hawke was nowhere to be seen.

CB&O

Jessica eyed the water longingly and made up her mind that after dark she would sneak down to bathe in a pool the bend in the stream created. For now though it would supply her with dinner and a moment of peaceful beauty. Water trickled in a soothing rhythm. Flowers dotted the mossy bank. A light breeze gently stirred the leaves overhead. It was perfect.

All her chores were completed and the next day was Sunday, a day of rest. After a month and a half on the trail, she looked forward to the days of rest. Mr. Richmond was their acting preacher, and he did a wonderful job. Everyone in the wagon train attended services. His sermons tended to be uplifting. After that there would be a potluck dinner. Then there would be singing, followed by Mr. Ford bringing out his fiddle and there would be dancing.

Jessica wished she could join the dancing, but everyone thought she was a boy so there was no way since she had no desire to dance with a woman, especially Olivia Freeman. She was only a year older then Olivia, and hoped all they had in common ended at the close proximity of the ages.

The girl was spoiled, pouty, useless, and irritating to say the least. She was also quite pretty, well, very beautiful. Jessica had watched her flirt with Nathan Hawke, but to give him credit, he didn't acknowledge it. He would tip his hat politely and go on his way.

He had danced with Olivia last Sunday, but he had danced with every woman in the company except her, but she couldn't hold that against him. The image of her dancing with Nathan Hawke rushed through her mind taking her breath with it. She tried to shake it off, but it lingered with a wave of heat. The man was too … she couldn't put the words together even in her mind. He disturbed her and she didn't like it.

She had avoided him since she had awakened in his wagon. She never should have crawled into the wagon. It was foolish. What would happen if it was ever discovered that she was a woman? She would be ruined. Her mother would be horrified.

The thought of her mother brought a wave of different

images, Clifford Raker. She wondered if the memories of him would ever fade. There was one nice thing about being exhausted at the end of the day. She was often too tired to have nightmares of him. She just wished they would go away entirely. She was far away and safe from him.

A twig snapped behind her. Jessica sprang up then muffled a scream when her eyes met the dark brown ones set wide in the child's face.

"Hey, Jess," Jonathan Hammond greeted in his ever cheerful voice.

"Jon, you scared me." She forced out, once she could get her breath.

"Momma said I could watch you fish if I wasn't botherin' you."

Jessica managed another deep breath. "No, you're not bothering me." A shiver of released energy rippled over her body. Jessica decided she could use the distraction from her own thoughts. And open, good-hearted Jon made a great distraction.

"Have you caught anythin' yet?"

"No, I was just resting a minute before I got started." She picked up the willow she had trimmed down and tied a string on. Jessica flicked the string in the water upstream and let it drift down into the deep pool off the bank in front of her. Jon moved forward and settled on the bank next to her.

"I stopped and saw your horses on the way here. Ruby is going to have her colt soon isn't she?"

"Anytime now."

At first, Jessica had tried to avoid the boy just like she did everyone else but it was no use. There was no avoiding Jonathan Hammond. The inquisitive six-year old was just always there. It didn't take her long to fall in love with the boy who openly accepted her as she was. "She's restless this evening, that could mean it's getting close."

"Papa said he would help if you needed it."

Jessica nodded. "Mr. Garfield and Mr. Hawke offered too."

"I'd have Mr. Hawke help. Papa's good with horses but Mr. Hawke talks to them. Papa says he's never seen a man who can handle horses like Mr. Hawke."

Jessica was about to answer when her pole dipped. She jerked up and managed to keep the fish on the hook.

"Hey, you got one." Jon jumped to his feet, dancing around as she swung it to the bank. About a foot long, the brown fish with bright orange spots was the perfect size for her dinner.

"Can we catch some more?" Jon asked excited.

"Would you like fish for dinner?"

The boy nodded. "Mama would like some fresh fish, but Papa and Joseph are helping Mr. Garfield work on Mr. Ford's wagon tongue."

"Then it looks like it's up to you to bring home dinner." A minute later Jessica flipped the hook back in the water and handed the pole over to Jon.

The boy nestled to her side. "You think Ruby will have her colt tonight?"

Jessica smiled. The boy was back to his favorite topic. "It's a quite possibility. It would be nice. Then I wouldn't have to worry about holding up the wagons at all or being left behind." Jessica had been wondering about the possibility all afternoon since she'd noticed Ruby's restlessness. Having about made up her mind to stop on her own, she had been relieved when the wagons pulled up early.

She staked Ruby off by herself to give her room just in case. Ruby seemed fine when she checked on the horse one last time before she'd come down to fish. A thrill ran through her at the thought of a new foal.

"How's fishing?"

Again, Jess had to fight to keep in a scream as she twisted around. The deep male voice was familiar, but she wasn't expecting it. It had seemed that Nathan Hawke had been avoiding her as much as she was avoiding him.

In the last three days, the only words she'd said to him were a quick thank you for the use of his wagon, which he brushed aside. She felt a brief flash of pain at the thought of him ignoring her. As far as she knew, she'd done nothing to insult him. Jessica decided it was better for her to keep her distance. She just wished that she could do the same with Emery Hayes

Hayes had received a strict warning from the wagon master about drinking and had been assigned extra watches, which left him down right mad, and most of his anger was directed at her. He hadn't really done anything outright, just some crude cutting remarks and bumping into her a couple times with enough force that he about knocked her over as he passed. Jessica felt her unease growing and tried harder to avoid the man.

Jon spoke up, giving her time to catch her breath and reorganize her thoughts. "Hey, Mr. Hawke, Jess caught one already. I just started fishin'. I'm going to catch enough for dinner."

"That sounds good. I'm going to give it a try myself. I'll move just a little farther upstream."

"Ruby is going to have her colt tonight," Jon spoke up with his ever present youthful exuberance.

"Is that so?" He turned his attention to Jess for verification.

"I'm not certain. She's just acting restless and shifting around a lot. She also doesn't seem interested in eating."

"I'll stop by and check on her after supper." It was a cross between an offer and a statement.

It was her first instinct to turn him down, but Jon was right. There was no one with them better with horses than Nathan. "I would be grateful." She could tell by his reaction that he was surprised by her acceptance of the help.

"I'll be by then." He nodded and moved off up the stream.

Jessica had a hard time taking her eyes off the man's long legged stride. There was something in his walk.

"Do you like Mr. Hawke?" Jon asked.

Jess jerked at the question, spinning back to face the boy. Then realized he couldn't be meaning the same thing that she had thought he meant.

She managed to nod. "Mr. Hawke is a good man. And as you said, he's good with horses."

"Olivia Freeman is making calf eyes at him. Mama says the girl is shameless because he's obviously not interested in her. I think she's sick. I wouldn't want her either. She doesn't like horses and she's never gone fishing. She mostly just sits around while her parents work."

Jess wasn't sure what to say to that. She had noticed the same thing but couldn't figure why Jon was pointing it out to her. Luckily, she was saved from answering when the pole Jon was holding dipped violently.

"I got a fish!" Jon cheered so loud Jessica wouldn't be surprised if they could have heard him back at camp.

◌◐◑◌

Jessica ran her hand over Ruby's neck, along her back then down over her extended stomach. She felt the muscles tighten and clench. There was no doubt about it. The mare was in labor. "It's all right, girl," Jessica soothed the horse. "It's going to be just fine." She prayed it would be so.

Most labors went smooth, but there was always a chance. She wished her father or Amos, were there. They knew what to do if things went wrong.

"How's she doing?"

This time the wave of relief that ran over Jessica washed away the startled reaction to the man walking up behind her. Jessica looked back grateful to see Nathan Hawke. "She seems good. She's definitely in labor."

The man moved forward greeting the horse, then ran

his hand over the mare in much the same way she'd just done. He nodded. "It'll be awhile yet but before the night is over you should have a new foal." He took his attention from the horse and looked over to her. "You all right?"

She nodded. It was her first instinct to wave the question off, instead she found herself answering. "It's just … I've never had one of my horses deliver on my own. I'm worried if something goes wrong."

"I'll be here. I'm pretty good with horses, if I do say so myself."

"I know, I didn't mean … thank you for the help. I'm just concerned. I haven't been letting Ruby rest up much with our traveling. I mean, the pace has been easy, and I've taken care of her, but it's not like she was in her pasture back at The Meadows. Maybe I should have left her and Slippers behind."

"Don't worry. The mares are fine. As you said, the trail hasn't been difficult. You haven't been putting packs on them. The exercise is good for yhem. I've watched you. You do a good job tending them."

"I know. It's just that I worry, and there's so much I haven't been able to do for her."

"You sound like an old-maid twittering around, boy. Just relax and let nature take its course. If it needs a little help, we'll worry about it then."

"That's about what my father would tell me. But I was always there pacing and watching. He told me once, when I have my own baby, I'll be so busy making sure that everything is perfect and ready for it that someone would have to tell me when it was time to just have it."

Nathan started to laugh, and Jessica realized what she'd just said. Luckily, he didn't seem to take it as her father meant it, as her being so busy and not a wife. She was just so jittery. What was wrong with her? "I'm going to check on Slippers."

03☙

Nathan watched as Jess moved over to the other horses to where the mare, that would be in the same position in another week or so, stood. He smiled again at Jess. The boy took his responsibilities like a man. He wondered how the boy would be when he had his own child. He was good with Jonathan. The boy was always hanging around Jess. He had slid past Jess' guard where no one else had been able to.

Nathan smiled again but this time at the thought of the younger boy. He'd like to have a son one day like Jon. He felt a wash of envy. He really should have taken a wife before he left. He knew women were scarce out west.

He just couldn't seem to choose a wife from the women in the area. None seemed right to him. Every time he thought of it, he had gotten an awful sinking feeling in his gut, like he would be missing something. He shook his head dislodging the thoughts. Maybe there would be a widow woman waiting for him out in California.

He turned his attention back to the mare, running his hand down over her. "It won't be long now, girl. You're doing real fine, even if you do have Jess anxious. Maybe I'll fetch my bedroll and bring it over here. There's always a chance the smell of fresh birth will attract wild animals, even with this many people around, but we better not mention that to Jess. He's too nervous already." For a minute he watched the boy-man that was such an enigma to him.

The mare settled into the grass just after the sun disappeared behind the mountains and the fiery color faded from the sky. Jessica hung a lantern from a tree branch burning some of her precious oil. Her concern wasn't on the oil, though. She stroked the mare's head and focused on the man who knelt by the mare's heaving side.

Nathan again slid his hands over the animal, talking softly. Jessica could hear the tension in his voice.

"There's something wrong, isn't there?" She could no

longer keep back the question. Ruby threw up her head in an effort to rise, postponing the answer as both humans moved to settle the horse.

"I'm afraid the foal's either turned or caught up in there."

Jessica felt waves of sickness. Fear attacked her. Leaning over, she pressed her face into her mare's velvety neck, fighting back tears. "I shouldn't have brought her."

"This has nothing to do with the journey. It could've happened just as easily back in her stable. We're just going to have to help her a little. We need to get the foal out, or we'll lose both of them." There was a firm reassurance in his voice that Jessica tried to cling to. "I'm going to need your help. I'm going to have to reach in and try to get a hold of the foal and help ease it out. I need you to lie over her neck and try to keep her down. In fact, maybe you better get Mr. Sanders or Hammond to add some more weight."

Jessica sat back, brushing away the moisture on her cheeks. "Mr. Sanders should just be going off watch. I'll ask if he can come."

Glad for something to do, she jumped up to get the man. He had passed by several times to check on them in the last two hours. She knew what Nathan was going to do. She had seen her father and Amos do it before. Jessica felt a wave of fear. If Nathan couldn't get the foal, she would lose both it and Ruby. If he could get the foal out in time, there was a chance he could save them both. She felt a surge of hope. Nathan was good with horses.

Jessica ran into Mr. Sanders before she neared the wagons. The man had been coming their way. He quickened his pace when Jessica told him what was happening. Nathan was taking off his shirt when they approached.

"Jess, you take her head and try to keep her calm." Nathan gave instructions. "Andrew, can you add weight to her neck? We don't want the horse trying to stand."

The older man nodded, and they all moved into position.

"Easy, Ruby." Jessica stroked the mare's nose then kept up the constant banter, trying to keep the mare from kicking Nathan. Jessica again buried her head against the mare, but this time it was so she couldn't see what Nathan was doing.

He, too, was talking calmly to the horse. Ruby jerked and Nathan's voice broke off with a grunt then, he continued. "That's it, doing fine."

Jessica raised her head enough to see him. The glow of the lantern cut across the sheen of sweat on him even though the night was cool. His muscles flexed. Jessica looked away, pressing her cheek back to Ruby's. "That's it." His voice dropped to a relieved tone, and Jessica raised her head in time to see him slide out his hand with a pair of glistening hooves.

Jessica watched as Nathan sat back, his arm covered with mucus, but his eyes fixed on the horse. He looked satisfied, and Jessica felt a wave of hope. She followed his gaze over to Ruby and saw the mare's sides heave. Mr. Sanders sat back also as the stomach muscles of the mare tightened again.

A tiny nose appeared then a moment later the foal slid all the way out. Nathan leaned forward to rub the slime away from the colt's nose. Jessica caught her breath as the mare pulled herself up and joined him in the cleaning of the colt. Tears flowed from Jessica's eyes when the colt moved under his mother's tongue.

"You did it." Mr. Sanders voiced her thoughts.

"I just had to get him going the right way. Let's move back and give mama some room."

Jessica moved back with the men, finally taking her eyes from the new colt to look at Nathan. "Thank you." She knew tears still trickled done her cheeks, but didn't care.

He had saved the colt and likely Ruby.

Nathan just nodded, as if he was uncomfortable with her praise. He busied himself wiping down his arm and chest with his bandana.

"Here, I have a bath sheet you can use." She reached for the sheet she'd left hanging from the tree under the lantern.

"A ... thanks. I'll go to the creek to wash up." He took the cloth and moved off. Jessica watched him for a second before shifting her eyes back to the colt, who was stirring more animatedly now.

"Well, Jess, thanks to Nathan, you have a good looking colt there."

Jessica nodded, "Thank you for your help, Mr. Sanders."

"You're welcome. Glad it turned out right. Goodnight."

"Goodnight, thank you again." The man waved her off as he headed back toward the wagons.

☙

Nathan splashed another handful of the chilly water up over his skin and tried again to get the picture of Jess right in his mind. It just didn't want to come out the way it should. With the hat pushed back, the lantern light cutting across his face and the tears damping his eyelashes, Nathan could have sworn it was a woman standing there. He doused his arm with another handful of water.

It had to be the tears and the boy being so emotional. He had to give the boy a break. He was young, and the horses obviously meant a great deal to him. Nathan knew Jess thought he was going to lose the horse, then to have the mare fine plus a new colt was an exciting thing, but Jess really needed to toughen up or someone would give him a hard time.

Pushing the knowledge that Jess was a boy firmly into his mind, he stood and dried off. Dang the toweling even smelled good. Nathan stared down at it for a second before he continued. He was going insane thinking a toweling sheet could smell feminine. But, as he hung it around his neck, he again could have sworn it did. Maybe it was left over from Jess' mother, he thought as he moved back toward where the horses were tethered.

Jessica was still staring at the mare and her foal when she heard Nathan return. The colt was working to get his shaky legs under him. Nathan joined her watching the wonder. After a few comical attempts, the colt managed to make it up.

"That's it. He's got it now. He's a good looking colt, good size." Nathan commented.

"He looks like his sire, my father's horse. I was hoping at least one of the foals would be a colt. If he takes after my father's, he will be an incredible stallion."

"It looks like you have an excellent chance," Nathan commented as the colt wobbled its way to his mother to nurse.

"Yes." Jessica final turned her attention from the horses. "Thanks to you, I don't know what I would have done if you hadn't been here. I've seen my father do that before but I'm not sure I could have. I could have lost them both. I don't know how to thank you, Mr. Hawke."

"It's Nathan, and I was glad to help," he paused. "But, I wouldn't object to a few meals sent my way if you prepare a little extra."

"It's the least I can do."

"Well, here I better give this back to you." Nathan reached up pulling the bath sheet from around his neck.

Again the lantern light slid over his bare skin, but this time Jessica was mesmerized by it. Her breath caught at the sight of him. He was a beautifully built man. Well sculptured by hard work. A sprinkling of hair showed on his chest drawing her attention. Jessica realized she wanted to reach out and touch it, wondering if would be coarse or soft. Heat flooded her cheeks.

Jessica spun away, forcing her attention to the horses. "I better shut down the lantern so they can get some sleep. It's been a big day for them."

"Yes, I'll be just over there if you need anything."

"We'll be fine now. Goodnight." She busied herself hanging the toweling up, taking a lot longer than necessary.

"Night."

Behind her, she heard him move off. She waited a minute then went to check on the other horses. One last check on Ruby and her colt then Jessica turned down the lantern and climbed into her bedroll.

Chapter Six

"Oh, wow, Jess. Ruby had her foal."

Jess opened her eyes and winced at the bright sun. "Morning Jon." She turned her head to see Ruby contently munching in the tall grass with the colt nursing. His wobbly legs much steadier. The sun glistened off his ebony coat. He was beautiful, just like his sire. She uttered a prayer of thanks for his life. "He was born last night with the help of Mr. Hawke."

The boy nodded in a knowing way. "What's his name?"

"I haven't even thought of that yet." She sat up, running her fingers through her hair and reached for her hat, placing it on her head. "Tell you what, why don't you come up with some ideas for me to pick from, then I'll decide on one."

"You mean it? I can help name him?"

"Sure." Jessica pushed back her bedding and pulled on her boots. "Have you met the colt yet?"

Jon shook his head, excitement lit his face.

"Well, let's go congratulate Ruby and say hello." Jessica led the way. They stopped by the mare letting her sniff them before working their way around her side to the colt. At first touch, the colt shied. They waited while the colt's natural curiosity got the best of him, and he edged over to investigate the humans. He jumped but with soothing words and patience he settled down and enjoyed the attention.

Jessica laughed as the colt butted Jon. The two were

about the same height and each showed the same curiosity of the other. Jessica rubbed her hand over the colt until it decided it had had enough of the boy and went back to nursing.

"Time to leave them alone," Jessica said after a minute more and waited for the boy to take one last pet.

They had just moved away when Jon's mother came hurrying toward them. "Jon what are you doing bothering Jess for?"

"Ruby had her colt."

Jon's mother shifted her gaze and her face softened at the foal. "I see. Well, that's good, but you need to have some breakfast. It will soon be time for services."

"Oh, but Mama."

"You need to eat and not be pestering Jess."

The boy started to groan again but Jessica cut him off. "He's no trouble. I didn't realize it was so late. I slept in." Jess turned her attention back to Jon. "Why don't you run and get something to eat, then after services you can come back and see if we can come up with a name for him."

The boy beamed back to his mother. "I get to help name him."

"Do you now. Well, that's something special, isn't it?"

"I better go eat. Bye Jess." Jon ran back through the meadow.

"I'm sorry about him bothering you." The woman gave a smile and shrugged her shoulders. "The horses."

"I've told you before, he's no trouble."

"I know you say so, but if he ever becomes a problem, let me know.

"I will, but he's honestly no trouble." Jessica knew the woman had her hands full keeping track of Jon's little brother, four other children and her husband being the wagon master."

"Well, thank you again, Jess. Stop by if you'd like some breakfast. We have some left. There's no need for you to try to prepare something this late."

"I will. Thank you. I need to wash first."

"That's fine. I'll leave it out for you." The woman headed back to the wagons.

Jessica picked up the water bucket so she could fill it when she took the other horses down to the stream. Once they were watered, she moved up stream to wash. She was on the way back when she heard someone moving her direction through the trees. Branches snapped as they were pushed aside. The footsteps were heavy and uneven. Jessica froze, and then groaned inwardly when Emery Hayes moved into sight.

The man noticed her and a sneer crested his lips. "So you have another horse."

"Yes." Jessica wasn't sure what to make of his contempt.

"It better not slow us up."

"It won't. The wagons are slow enough."

The man snorted. Jessica thought he'd move away, but he just stood there eyeing her. Jessica fought to stand up under his stare. "They better not. I saw you whining to Hawke last night. He coddles you too much. Your pa should've beat it out of you. I would've. Then you wouldn't be such a sniveling whelp."

Jessica stood her ground, determined not to tremble though his words sickened her.

Hayes made another snorting sound and stomped away, stumbling a little as he went. Jessica wondered if he'd been drinking again. She then discounted it because he couldn't have that much alcohol with him to keep drinking that often. Still, she couldn't stomach the man.

She shuddered at the thought of him as a father. There was no doubt by the way he spoke of beating a child that he would do just that. With a shiver, she headed over to the Hammonds wagon for the promised breakfast, feeling a wave of relief that she didn't have to make it herself.

ೞ৪০

"Jess." Jon ran toward her. Jessica was getting used to the boy's constant visits. He spent as much time as possible with her and the colt. She smiled at how serious he'd taken the responsibility of naming the colt. He discarded the names Midnight and Blacky the first day as being too plain. "What do you think of Samson and Goliath or Coal? He's kind of small to think of him being big enough for a Samson or Goliath, but he'll grow, and they're tough names. And I just like Coal."

Jessica was quiet a second. "I think I like the name Coal. His sire was my father's horse, and his name was Smokey. It seems kind of fitting to go with Coal."

"You really like it?" His eyes were the size of silver dollars with hopeful excitement and Jessica thought again. "I do."

This time Jon thought, then nodded. "I do too. It's a good name for him."

She had to fight back a laugh.

"Mr. Hawke," Jon called out the name, startling her. "We named the colt."

"That's good. What's the name?"

"Coal. Jess said that his sire's name was Smokey, so likes it."

"That does seem to fit. I see you're helping Jess keep good track of him."

The boy nodded then eyed the knife in the man's hand. "What are you doing?"

"I got a sliver in my hand and was going to dig it out."

"With a knife," Jessica couldn't keep the shock from her voice. "Don't do that. Let me see." She didn't even think before reaching for his hand. It was a large sliver that had broken off at the surface. "We need a needle to lift that up. Wait a minute." Jessica went to her packs and rifled around a moment.

"Here hold this." She handed him the needle and

pulled off her glove. "All right, let me see." She took back the needle, and then laid her hand on his, turning it so she could get a better look. Jessica stepped forward bracing his arm against her side to steady it. "Hold still," she cautioned, just before she gently caught the edge of the sliver to work it up.

"Let me see your knife," she said after a moment of working with it.

Nathan said nothing as he handed the knife over. Jessica placed the edge of the knife under the sliver then pinched down on it with the tip of her fingernail, drawing her hand back, slowly as the sliver slid out intact.

"Mr. Hawke, are you injured?" Jess recognized Olivia Freeman's voice without turning. The forced sweetness in it was sickening.

"No, Miss Olivia, just a sliver."

"You should have it tended."

"Jess is doing it."

The young woman made a shooing motion, moving forward. "You don't want a boy with clumsy fingers to do it. Let me see. I'll be happy to do it for you. I promise I have a much softer touch."

"Actually, it's all done." Jessica had to fight to keep her voice down.

Jon was right about the way Olivia Freeman 'goo'd' over Nathan, it was sickening.

"Oh, I better make sure." Olivia reached for Nathan's hand.

"It's fine. Thank you, Jess. Bye, Jon." He flicked the brim of the boy's hat and nodded to the young woman. "Miss."

Jessica tried to hide her smile as she watched Olivia stare after him. The woman stamped her foot, sent a glare over her shoulder then with a flip of her hair, she flounced away.

Jon looked up and made a gagging motion that almost

broke free the laughter that Jessica was holding back. When the young woman disappeared, a wave of laughter rolled out and was joined with Jon's.

Jessica shook her head, smiling down. The boy was precious.

ᘓᙅᘔᐛ

It was late and Nathan knew he should be asleep but once again sleep wouldn't come, and once more it was because his thoughts were focused on Jess Wells. He could still remember the feel of Jess' hands on his.

When Jess pulled off the glove, he could hardly hold back exclaiming about how delicate his hands were. He wondered what Olivia Freeman would say if he said that Jess had softer, more delicate hands. He wished he could forget how tender the touch had been. The feel when Jess held his arm against his body.

It was a womanly thing to do. He knew Jess did it because that was undoubtedly how his mother did it, but still. He wished Jess was a woman. It would make things right. He wouldn't be laying here debating his sanity. He could be sleeping, not thinking about how a boy had the sweetest most feminine scent that had ever stirred his scenes.

No, that wasn't right. The scent had to be from Jess' mother. Maybe he should tell Jess he should quit using his mother's soap. That would be better. He closed his eyes and willed his mind to clear.

Chapter Seven

"Jess, look, there are riders coming." Jon's excited voice drew her attention up. "Who do you think they are?" He was already on his feet, headed for his father, who would go out and meet the two approaching men.

All the relaxation was gone from her body. It'd been over four weeks since they had left all signs of civilization. Until that point every moment she'd been afraid her stepfather would find her or that he'd send someone after her, but each day she began to feel safer.

Now her fear resurfaced. Pulling her hat low, she rose and stepped back into the trees. She warily watched from the shadows, barely able to hear the men.

"Permission to approach?" One of the riders yelled out.

"Come away," Mr. Hammond called back. "What can I do for you?" Jacob Hammond asked as the men approached.

Jess didn't recognize either of the men and relaxed a little until they spoke.

"Just wondering about getting some supplies and some fresh horses? I see some nice stock over there."

Jess went back on alert.

"Sorry we can't offer you much in the way of supplies. I'm sure you can understand." The wagon master said, "Just a few staples."

"What about the horse flesh? Who do they happen to belong to?" A sharp featured man with heavy whiskers asked.

"As for the horses, they're not for sale." There was

firmness in Hammond's voice that wasn't normally there. Jess realized then he'd taken a dislike to the men. She noticed that Nathan had also moved closer adding his support.

"You're the owner then? We'll give you a fair price." One of the men pressed, looking between Hammond and Hawke.

"They're not for sale." This time it was Nathan that answered.

"Then you're the owner."

"They belong to one of the other men, but he's already been asked and doesn't want to sell."

"We'd like to ask for ourselves if you don't mind. Maybe we can make a better offer," the man pushed.

Hammond hesitated slightly. "If you wish, that would be Jess Wells. Jon." He looked down at his son. "Will you go find Jess please?"

The boy nodded and tore off.

"Where are you all from?" the other man asked good-naturedly.

"Out of Clearwater ourselves, most are from the area round about. Where you from?" Mr. Hammond returned the question.

"Springville."

"Where are you headed?" Nathan moved closer to the wagon-master.

"West," the whiskered man said simply

"Any information you might have for us?" Mr. Hammond asked.

"Not much. We've passed two wagon trains behind you, each about two days apart. One got held up at the last river crossing."

Attention was diverted to the pair approaching. Jon skipped forward. Jess hung back. She watched for signs of recognition. There didn't seem to be any, but one of the men narrowed his eyes on her.

"Jess, this is Mr. Jack and Stubbs. They want to know if you're interested in selling some horses." Mr. Hammond said bluntly, not waiting for the men to speak.

Jess knew she'd have to come forward, straightening herself up as tall as she could and lengthening her stride with mock confidence, she moved to the group, but kept her head tilted down so her hat brim left her face in shadow.

"They're not for sale." She kept her voice low.

The men turned her way and looked doubtingly at her. "Where's your pa boy?"

"Gone, the horses are mine and they're not for sale."

"You haven't even heard the price."

"It doesn't matter. They're not for sale."

"Where'd a young'un like you get horse flesh like those?"

"I raised them with my father before he died."

Jess didn't notice that Nathan had shifted behind her until she felt a hand rest on her shoulder.

"He said they're not for sale. That's final."

There was a pause. "What about that stallion over there?" The man shifted and pointed to where Titan was tied away from the mares.

"He's mine and he's not for sale either," Nathan answered. The hardness in his voice left no doubt the discussion was over. Still the men eyed them for a moment more, staring at Jess then the horses.

Finally the one that had done most of the talking spoke up. "Well," he drawled out. "I guess we'll be on our way then, there's still plenty of light yet."

Together they turned and rode off, leaving everyone behind them standing silent as they watch them disappear into the distance.

Nathan was the one who broke the silence. "We might want to put extra guards on tonight."

Jessica spun to look at him and saw Jacob Hammond

nodded.

"You think they'll be back?" There was a hitch in her voice.

"I think it's more than a possibility. They didn't bother trying to get the supplies we offered."

Mr. Hammond continued with another nod. "What they were really interested in were the horses. You have some good looking animals, Jess. A man could get quite a bit for them, especially out here on the trail where the gettin's hard."

"Don't worry so." Nathan patted her shoulder. "We'll keep all the horses closer in tonight just to be on the safe side."

"What about Lady and Titan?"

"We'll just have to take a chance. If it happens, it happens and odds are it will. You ought to feel fortunate. I hope to get quite a large stud fee out of him some day. He's a great horse. Maybe we better talk stud fee."

Jess knew he was only semi-serious. That he was more teasing her to try to get her to relax.

♋

The evening passed without incident, the only problem was Emery Hayes' grumbling about the extra watches. When it was time to sleep, Jessica couldn't rest. She should've been tired, for the last two nights she'd drawn the third watch. Tonight was to be her rest night. Instead, she slid from her bedroll and pulled on her boots.

She crossed the edge of the camp toward the horses. She paused, announcing her presence to Mr. Sanders so he would know she was there. She didn't want to get shot just because she was restless. Mr. Sanders and his wife were the oldest couple of the group. He was a blacksmith and had plenty of strength in his body but was a quiet man. Jessica liked him and his wife, a well-rounded woman with a big heart.

"I'm going to walk down and check on the horses," she

said coming up to him.

"I was just over there. They're a bit skittish but fine. That stallion of Hawke's is sure interested in that filly of yours. You ought to just let it get done with so he'll settle down."

"I might have to, but she'll be out of season in a couple more days. I'd sooner be where I could set some cautions."

"Well, that may be, but you could probably get a mighty fine looking foal. He's a right proud stallion, and she's one sweet filly with a lot of spunk. That combination is hard to beat."

Jessica nodded again. She knew it was true. She'd been thinking of it. Maybe Nathan would help her set up things after they made camp tomorrow night. They could cover Titan's hooves with some canvas. They could also tie Lady so she wouldn't be able to kick out and fight him. That would be the best.

"I'll approach Mr. Hawke about it tomorrow."

The old man nodded. "I'll give a hand if you need."

"Thank you, I'd appreciate it. I'm going to check on them before I turn in."

"You take care of your animals. That's good." The man nodded again in approval.

She smiled at him. "Goodnight, Mr. Sanders." Jessica walked away knowing she would talk to Hawke in the morning, feeling comfortable now that she had made the decision. She would even offer him a stud fee. It was only fair. Mr. Sanders was right. A colt or filly sired by Titan promised to be an excellent animal.

Jessica heard the nervous whinnying of the horses before she drew close. Mr. Sanders was right about that too. They were skittish.

She was almost to the horses when a commotion and angry snort from Nathan's stallion hastened her steps. Jessica heard a faint curse. Then from the sliver of light from the moon, she could see a man struggling with the halter on Titan.

"Stop!" she yelled, charging forward without thought. "Help," she screamed the alarm, spooking the horses more than they already were.

Jessica had her attention on the man she saw and didn't even notice the blow that caught her from the side. One instant she was upright and alert, moving and ready to fight, the next moment she hit the ground, stunned, but fortunately she'd just caught a glancing blow because she was moving.

"Hurry."

She heard from above her.

"Let's get out of here. I have the stallion, just forget the others."

"Titan!" Jessica couldn't let them take Nathan's horse. She staggered to her feet, not hearing the activity in the camp. She focused on the man in front of her trying to pull himself up into the saddle while holding onto the lead rope of the frightened stallion.

"No!" If her mind hadn't been clouded from the blow she might have realized what a bad idea it was, but as it was, she could only concentrate on one thing, and that was getting Titan.

Jessica lunged, grabbing at the man. He threw back his elbow catching her in the shoulder. Pain shocked her, but she refused to go down. Her hand caught and clung to the saddle. With one hand, she clawed at the man, but he made it onto the horse's back.

In the faint light, Jessica saw his hand swing out toward her, but she was saved from the blow as Titan reared back almost pulling the man off his horse. The man's attention shifted from her to trying to get the lead rope around the saddle horn to secure the stallion. Jessica grabbed at his hands fighting for the rope, trying to hang on as his horse danced around nervously, as did Titan.

At one point the animals collided, pinning Jessica

between them, knocking the air from her body, cutting off her cry. Then Titan pulled back. Free, Titan tore across the meadow. Above her, the man swore, kicking out. His booted foot caught her in the ribs. Jessica cried out, releasing the saddle, but her hand was wedged between the thick leather and the horse's body.

"Let's get out of here," yelled one of the men. The man gave another kick but this time it was to get his horse moving. Trapped, Jessica was slammed against the side of the horse, the stirrup and boot catching her again in her lower ribs. Her feet went out from under her. Jessica felt as if her arm was being torn from her body then she was falling. She hit the ground and tumbled.

Pain waved over her. She could hear shouts and curses, but she didn't care about anything except trying to get air into her burning chest. She lay still, unable to move from pain, trying to cling to consciousness which her mind insisted she needed, though she wished for oblivion from the pain.

She heard more yelling that solidified into familiar voices. There was a command for someone to get the horses settled. Then a shrill whistle broke the air that was followed shortly by an angry snort of a horse.

Even in her fogged mind, she realized Titan was still close by.

The voices also seemed to be closer, but she couldn't manage to call out. Jessica heard a voice that was so soothing it calmed her, though she knew Nathan was talking to Titan. Jessica wanted to call out but could only force a groan past her lips.

Chapter Eight

Nathan was jerked out of sleep by the first yell and had his pants and boots on before the scream for help. He hit the ground running, heading for the horses and the direction of the yelling. He saw Sanders lumbering from the other side of the camp.

In the distance, he could make out the riders struggling with a horse that he recognized as Titan. The stallion wanted nothing to do with them, then Nathan saw the smaller figure, that he knew immediately was Jess.

Jess rushed one of the men just as he tried to mount his horse. Nathan was too far away to stop the kick that caught the boy then he lost sight of Jess in the mass of bodies, horses and shadows. Nathan drew his gun, shooting a warning shot in the air, knowing at that distance and on a full run he could as easily hit Jess or Titan.

The struggle continued, and then Nathan saw Titan break free. The horse tore off but swung back toward the mares. Then the riders took off. Behind him, Nathan heard more people coming from the wagons. He didn't slow his pace until he neared the already unsettled horses.

"Easy," Nathan murmured softly settling them as he moved among them. "Easy there." He caressed each animal as he passed doing a quick head count. They were all there. A sigh escape him.

He gave a loud whistle which Titan immediate answered. The stallion hadn't gone far, and now that the men were gone, his attention was turned to Jess' mare.

"I wouldn't think of it, old boy. Jess is not sure he

thinks you're good enough for the lady."

Jess, the name hit him. He didn't see the boy. "Jess!" He turned to Sanders. "Have you seen Jess?"

The man looked around and shook his head. "He'd come down here to check on the horses. It was him who yelled the warning," the man affirmed what Nathan had already figured.

Nathan turned in what he thought was the direction that the men had fled. He'd gone about twenty-five feet before he made out the boy's shape lying in the tall grass. Nathan ran the last few feet to the still figure.

"Jess." He dropped down beside him, relieved that he could see he was alive in the faint moonlight.

A groan escaped the boy at the sound of his name.

"Easy," he said in much the same way he used with the horses. Eyes opened then closed tight with another gasp of pain.

"Hold still and just take shallow breathes." The counsel was probably unnecessary because that was all the boy could take. The breathing was more short pained gulps. Jess' eyes were closed and Nathan was afraid he was beginning to fade into unconsciousness. "Stay awake. Listen to me!" he ordered. "Of all the foolishness, what did you think you were doing?"

"Titan." The word came out a whisper, followed by another small sharp breath.

"Titan is not worth your life. They could've shot you." Nathan finished running his hands over all of Jess' limbs, satisfied that nothing was broken. He wasn't so sure about the boy's ribs, with his labored breathing. He prayed they weren't broken, cracked would be bad enough.

Nathan went to work on the buttons of the coat, getting it out of the way, he picked up the conversation. "Titan wouldn't have let them take him far anyway. I don't think I could get rid of him if I tried." Nathan was down to just one button on the vest when Jess started to become alert.

"No," Jess gasped, trying to grab his hands.

Nathan brushed Jess' hands aside and pushed the vest out of the way. "Hold still, I need to check your ribs." Nathan started to pull the shirt free of his trousers.

"No." Jess' voice cracked with pain, and his struggling came more pronounced as he fought to sit up.

"Easy, stay down. I'm afraid you might have a couple broken ribs. I need to check you out before I move you. Stay down." He struggled with the boy, pushing him down. "If your rib is broken, you could send it through your heart or lung."

His hands made it under Jess' shirt only to come into contact with another layer of material. And he realized that Jess kept his money tied to his body. He almost grinned at the bulky money belt. He fumbled for the ties.

"No," Jess objected again, but this time he fought harder to sit up.

"Stop," Nathan snapped back. "I'm not gonna steal your money but I have to look." His hands slid up trying to ease Jess back down. When he came into contact with skin, Nathan's whole world tilted. The smooth, silky skin might be explained away, but the contour of the narrow waist could not be.

No, it couldn't be. His mind yelled, but as his large hands fitted to the trim waist and continued up, there was no mistaking the flare to her ribcage. He knew for certain. Nathan stopped his probe when he came in contact with a ridge of material. He was still unable to take his hands away as his mind cataloged all he was feeling.

Under his hands Jess had stilled, staring up at him. The pain in her face was combined with something new. In the dark it was hard to tell what it was but Nathan figured that it might be fear.

With all his ricocheting emotions she better be afraid. She! He felt about to explode. It must have shown on his face because she started to talk as if her pain was forgotten.

"Nathan please, I can—"

"Don't say a word," he growled, not able to keep it back. "Not a word."

She opened her mouth again then closed it.

"Wise, I'm not through with you, but for now I need to check you before I move you." He shook his head to get himself back under control then started to finger her ribs.

She closed her eyes and turned her head away as he slid his hands along each rib. She made several grimaces of pain but didn't say anything. He continued until he was to the edge of the material again. Binding he surmised and decided it was better not to contemplate that area.

"So far as I can tell nothing seems to be broken. We'll have to check closer when we get some light. If we're lucky, they'll just be bruised then I won't have to wait so long to take you over my knee."

Jess' gaze swung back to him. She glared up but remained silent.

"I'm going to lift you now. If you can't stand the pain, let me know." His concern was at odds with his previous statement. "If necessary we can think of another way to move you."

As angry as he was he was still as gentle as possible, going slowly and stopping when she whimpered.

"I'm fine," she whispered through clinched teeth.

Nathan could make out a tear that trailed down her cheek, but he made no comment as he headed for the wagons.

He ignored the men milling around the area, some watching him, others checking on the horses and talking.

"You better have a good explanation and even then I may not be able to keep from tanning your hide."

"Don't threaten me."

"Quiet! I should've figured this out from the first. How could I have been so stupid? There were so many times. I should've gone with my instincts." They were at his wagon before he was done venting. "This may hurt."

"Can I help, Hawke?" Jacob Hammond came hurrying up.

"Yes, can you hold Jess then hand her up to me and send someone to get your wife."

"Joseph, go get your ma," the wagon master commanded as he accepted Jess.

Nathan climbed into the wagon and held out his arms. Someone came up with a lantern, the light lit up her pale face before Nathan reached back to take her. He felt a wave of concern. "Let's take this slow."

He could see Jess bite her lip to keep from crying out. Another tear trickled down her face, but she didn't even let out a whimper. Once he had her in his arms, he turned and carefully laid her out on the bed he'd left just minutes before.

Nathan lit his own lantern while she struggled to breathe and get settled. He turned to her. "I'm going to remove your boots."

She nodded.

He got them off without too much pain to her then moved up to kneel beside her. "Okay, let's see about your coat and vest." He reached to pull his knife from its sheath.

"No, don't cut them. They're new."

"I don't care if they're silk from the orient. They need to come off and the most painless way will be to cut them off."

"No."

"Look, I can try to stay close to the seams then you can sew them back up. Though it doesn't matter, you won't be wearing boy's britches anymore."

"You have no say about that." She glared up.

"It's not seemly," he grumbled, more knowing he really had no say and wondered why he had even brought it up. One good thing, it seemed to get her mind off the pain. He reached for his knife again.

"Don't even think about pulling that knife or I'll start screaming."

"Now that, is a threat I'd expect out of a woman, but you're hurtin' too much to get the air to make a decent squeak."

She just glared at him in silent challenge.

"Fine." He threw up his hands. "I'll try to take them off you. But at the first outcry, we do it my way."

"I can do it."

"Foolish," he muttered but raised her slightly to slide the bulky material from her shoulders. Pain etched its way across her face, sweat glistened on her brow, but she didn't make a sound. Nathan was glad for the fact that the garment was much too large. It made it easier to get it off, but the way her body trembled with pain when he laid her back, he wished he'd ignored her and just cut the coat away.

He didn't get time to contemplate what next as Mrs. Hammond pushed back the canvas and climbed in.

"They said that Jess was hurt."

He nodded in way of an answer not taking his eyes off of the young woman as he settled her down.

The pain had bleached all the color from her face and her breathing had turned labored. He prayed again she hadn't broken her ribs, either way, he was done with foolishness. "That's it," he forced out. "We do the vest my way."

She made a weak squeak when he pulled the knife from its sheath.

"Quiet!" Nathan commanded as he gently lifted her arm enough to slice down the seam.

Jess closed her eyes but the only sound that came from her was another hiss of pain.

"Where's he hurt?" Sara Hammond drew closer.

"Her ribs, a couple may be broken though I'm hoping they're just bruised. We may not be able to tell though until she gets her breath back. Will you be able to handle this on your own?"

"Certainly, but–"

"Then I'm going to leave her to you." It was the fourth time he'd used the feminine term and this time it seemed to register with the woman.

"Her?" Sara repeated.

But Nathan focused on the anguish filled eyes. For some reason he was sure this wasn't from pain. It was as if she was accusing him of betrayal. He shook it off.

"I have to check on the horses. I'll keep everyone out." Before anything else could be said, he swung his leg over the tailgate and slid from the wagon. The minute his feet hit the ground, he pulled the canvas flap over and tied it down.

Nathan braced his hands on the wood panel, dropping his head to take a couple breaths in an effort to calm himself. He didn't know where all the anger was coming from, but it raged in his every pore.

The little fool, what could she have been thinking, pretending to be a boy, trying to stop horse thieves? All the frustration she'd caused him. Making him wonder if he was losing his sanity, he should have known.

"Nathan, is Jess gonna be all right?" Jacob Hammond asked from behind him.

"Yeah, until I get my hands on her," he ground out.

"Now don't be too hard on the boy. He's probably already regretting his actions. That boy really loves his horses."

Nathan took a deep breath, lifted his head and turned back toward the wagon-master. "We need to talk." He walked off toward the horses leaving the man to follow him.

※※

Jessica wanted to call him back, to explain, but she couldn't force enough air into her fiery chest. Tears filled her eyes and she gasped as a sob tried to break free.

"Now, now, just short breaths and try to relax." Sara Hammond brushed a tear from her cheek. "That's good. Just relax. I need to open you shirt to check your ribs." The woman talked as she worked away the shirt. "So that's how you hid," she continued as she encountered the altered corset. "I need to get that out of the way. What is your name?"

"Jess … Jessica." She labored to get out, and then groaned from the effort.

"If I wasn't seeing this, I never would have believed it. You sure had me fooled, but why in great aunt Gurtie's name would you ever pretend to be a boy?"

"Only way," she cried out again.

"Stay still," Sara Hammond probed each of the ribs. "I don't think that any are broken, but it wouldn't surprise me if a couple here aren't cracked. You're going to be terribly bruised and won't be moving for several days. I would say it was a good thing you had yourself wrapped so, it's probably what saved you."

Jessica tried to focus on the woman's words.

"I'm going to have to bind your ribs. It'll hurt but it has to be tight in case some are broken, then you're going to have to remain still. Though you're going to have to sit up for a moment." The woman didn't hesitate in cutting a strip of cloth off one of Nathan's blankets.

Jess made it to a semi-sitting position with the woman's help, but as Sara Hammond cinched up the wrapping, Jessica couldn't keep in the cry, lights flashed in front of her eyes then faded into darkness.

Chapter Nine

Jessica's body jerked, sending a wave of pain ricocheting through her. She woke with a cry then fought to catch her breath. Above her the canvas was pushed back and a shaft of light cut in. The wagon jerked, but this time, she focused on the face glaring down at her.

"I would ask how you're feeling, but I can guess. I'm sorry about the ride, but we had to move out. I'll get you a drink."

Nathan turned away, and Jessica could hear him talking to Ezra Hammond, then she heard what she guessed was the boy stepping onto the wagon. This time when the canvas was pushed aside Nathan crawled in.

"Sara moved back to her wagon to get some rest after she sat up with you the rest of the night." He knelt beside her with his water skin in hand. "I'm going to raise you a little so you can drink."

Jessica realized as she shifted that she was wearing a nightgown buttoned to her chin. She fought back a groan as Nathan eased her up, but the water felt too blessed on her throat for her to care about the pain.

"More?"

She nodded and he tipped it back up.

"Good, I have a biscuit here for you if you think you can eat it."

"Yes, please." She wanted to ask him some questions, but from his forbidding demeanor, she knew he was still furious and decided against it.

"You should get some rest," he ground out, turning

away to crawl back through the opening.

Jessica felt an almost unbearable need to cry that had nothing to do with the flashes of pain produced by the constant movements of the wagon. She wanted to plead to Nathan not to be angry with her, which made her furious to care so much about what he thought.

She thought of going after him until the wagon hit another bump and pain slashed through her side. Frustrated, all she could do was lay back and worry about what would happen to her now that her secret was known. Surely, they wouldn't force her to leave in the middle of nowhere.

But they would be reaching a fort in about two weeks time. They may insist on leaving her there, especially if she couldn't do her share of the chores. Such foolishness. She couldn't be injured. She had to take care of her horses. Who had tended them this morning?

As soon as the thought crossed her mind, she knew the answer, Nathan had. He would make sure they were well cared for.

Again a wave of frustration flowed over her. Why did it always have to be him? She drew in as deep a breath as possible to calm her emotions only to be greeted with the smell of him and it hit her. She was in his wagon, his bed. She had to rely totally on Nathan Hawke.

"No," she whispered aloud. She would not rely on anyone. She could take care of herself. She would show them there was no reason to doubt her place on the wagon train.

Jessica forced herself up to a seated position, and then cried out as pain again jabbed through her side, taking with it her breath. Her head fell back as she fought to get air into her lungs. She was too afraid to move or even try to lie down.

"What do you think you're doing?" The words were barked out behind her. Then she felt a hand on her back and another locked onto her arm, easing her back against

Nathan Hawke's thigh.

ᏣᎦᏇᎥᏅ

Nathan wanted to yell at the woman, but that was nothing new. He had wanted to yell at her from the moment he found out she was a woman, but the pallor of her face kept the words back. When she let out a little sigh and her breathing stilled, he felt himself take a breath. Her cry had scared him to death.

"You should not be moving around." He kept his voice calm.

"I need to be up." She struggled to get the words out.

"You should've told me you need ... I will get one of the ladies to help you."

"No." She shook her head. "Have to see to my horses."

"Your horses are fine. Their stringer is tied to the back of my wagon."

"I need to—"

"You need to stay down."

She started to shake her head. "Can take care—"

"You could not even stand up in a light breeze right now. There's no way you can get on a horse."

"But—"

"Don't say a word." Nathan knew he probably sounded like a general giving out orders, but seeing her in pain tore at him. He was not aware that he had started to massage her shoulder until she relaxed back into his lap and sighed. Her eyes closed, and he realized she was falling asleep.

"No, Jessica, don't go to sleep yet." His tone dropped to a softness that surprised him. He took a deep breath, firming up his voice. "Let's get you some more to drink."

She opened her eyes, and he wished immediately she hadn't. Pain was evident in the blue pools. She accepted several more sips of water before leaning back in exhaustion. Her eyes closed again, and Nathan found himself holding a sleeping woman. Staring down, he fought against thinking about how much he liked it.

No, he was not going to think of Jessica any more then he thought of Jess, even if now it didn't make him feel odd. He was not going to get involved with her. Still, he watched her sleep a minute before he eased her back down. She stirred as he tucked the blanket around her, but stilled when he lightly touched her cheek. Nathan pulled his hand back once again, surprised at his own action. He was not going to get involved.

CԒՑD

Jessica awoke a while later as the wagon bumped over a particularly rocky section. She prayed it would soon end. She wanted to sit up again but after the last attempt she was hesitant to try.

Jess remembered Nathan there behind her. His touch on her shoulders had been so soothing. There had been no fear when he had touched her. After Clifford Raker, she'd wondered if she would feel comfortable if a man ever touched her again. Maybe it was a foolish thought, but she had wondered that more than once after coming out of a particularly bad nightmare.

"Hey, Jess." Jon's head peeked up over the tail gate of the wagon. "You're awake."

"Hello, Jon."

Dimples creased the blond boy's face as he climbed right in. "You should hear it. Everyone's talking about what happened. They figure it was those two guys that returned to steal the horses. And that they almost got Titan, but you stopped them."

Jessica bet they were talking about something else about her too, but Jon didn't seem concerned about that. He was off on another subject, his favorite one. "I kept an eye on Coal today. He stayed right by Ruby and was just fine. I helped Mr. Hawke tend them this morning when we stopped. They all settled right down."

"We're done for the day?" She realized then that the wagon was no longer moving.

"Yeah, they decided to stop because of a river crossing. It's late enough in the day they decided to wait and make the attempt in the morning after they cross a couple times with just horses. It looks like there are a couple of deep holes.

The canvas was pushed back again, but this time it was Sara Hammond. "Jon what are you doing bothering Jessica?" His mother shook her head, but there was no sternness in her voice.

"I just came to keep her company."

"Well, why don't you go gather me some more firewood."

"But—"

"Go on. I need to see to Jessica."

"Thanks for coming to visit me." Jessica quickly spoke up so he wouldn't get into trouble. "Will you come see me again?"

He nodded and slid from the wagon.

"You just need to send him away if he's bothering you." Sara settled beside her.

"He wasn't bothering me, honestly."

The woman shook her head, whether in disbelief or amazement Jessica was not sure. "Here's some broth. You need to keep up your strength."

"I need to get up."

"Nathan will be here shortly to help you up."

"No, I mean that I have to tend my horses."

"No, you don't. You're to stay down in bed. Do you hear me? Until the bruising and swelling goes down and we're sure you don't have a broken rib, you're not doing anything."

"But if I can't take care of my chores, what's going to happen?"

"Don't worry about that now. They aren't going to do anything until you're on your feet again. So just quit worrying."

"But–"

"No, you just listen to me and don't go borrowing trouble before you have to face it. Now it sounds like Nathan is here." Her words were affirmed when the canvas was pushed back again and Nathan climbed in.

"Are you ready?" he said in the way of greeting. When Sara nodded, he continued. "I guess the best way to do it is, if you can keep the blanket around you, I can try to lift you without causing you too much pain."

Before Jessica had time to answer, he leaned over and slid his arms under her. Startled, she threw her arms around his neck and clung to him as he rose.

"That's good, hold tight as I step down."

There was no other option for her. One minute they were in the wagon, the next she was in the bright late afternoon light. She blinked several times to adjust her eyes.

"This way." Sara led the way into the trees, and Jessica found herself being carried by Nathan Hawke.

"I can walk." She looked up only to receive a brief shake of his head. At Sara's direction, he placed her down and moved off, only to reappear when Sara called him again. A few minutes later, she was back in the wagon, settled down after something to eat.

Jessica found herself doing just what Sara told her to do the next day. When needed, Nathan carried her out of the wagon into the woods. Sara brought her food and sat with her. She also had brief visits the next day by Mrs. Sanders and Mrs. Garfield, and their preacher Mr. Richmond and his wife, did a brief stop. She thought they were all being very nice, but it was obvious they were not sure what to do with her. They were kind. The women promised to send food over and offered their help, if she needed anything.

That night after settling back in bed, Jessica started a conversation with Sara while she ate her dinner.

"Whose nightgown is this?"

"One of mine."

"Thank you for letting me wear it. I have one in my pack so I can give this back to you."

"We'll worry about that after you're up."

"I'd like to be up tomorrow."

"You'd better stay down another day. Then I'll try to find you a dress. The Freeman girl should be about the same size as you. I'm going to see if she has one that you can borrow."

"That won't be necessary. I have my own clothes in my packs." She tried not to think of the spoiled sixteen-year-old girl who had made several very obvious plays to get Nathan's attention. The girl was catty and shrewd. Jessica was glad that she wouldn't have to borrow anything from her. It would be easier if she could keep wearing her boy's clothes. They had some advantages over dresses. But she knew if she was going to be accepted in the train, she would have to change back to wearing a dress and acting more lady-like.

"I wouldn't plan on wearing your boy clothes just now," Sara echoed what she was thinking.

"I have dresses in my pack. That is if my packs got brought along." She felt a wave of unease. Surely they wouldn't leave them.

"Don't worry. Nathan took care of them."

Of course, Nathan took care of them. He had taken over everything in her life from the moment he figured out she wasn't a boy. He had even taken her money. The memory hit her with a shot of fear. How could she have forgotten? Anything could've happened to it.

No, she dampened her thoughts down. Nathan wouldn't have lost it and he was an honorable man. He would keep it safe. She didn't need to worry that he would steal it, but it was a lot of money. More than most people would see in their entire lives. She felt another wave of unease. If he claimed it there was no way she could prove that it was hers. No, a surge of trust wiped away any doubt. She trusted Nathan Hawke, but she would still ask him about the money.

"You're getting tired. You go to sleep now and I'll visit you first thing in the morning, then we'll talk more about getting dressed. But I wouldn't plan on getting up and dressed just yet. You're not ready. Give it a day or two more."

Unable to summon an argument, Jessica nodded. "I don't know how to thank you. I know I've been an imposition."

"We all have to look out for one another." The woman waved the gratitude away. "You're welcome."

"All you've done, it was very nice of you."

"Get some sleep."

Jessica planned on waiting until she could talk to Nathan Hawke when he came to get his belongings for the night but didn't get the chance, the instant the older woman climbed out of the wagon, she was asleep.

The next morning, the pain was again hardly bearable, and Sara gave her no option of getting dressed. She also didn't get to talk to Nathan because he was busy with the river crossing which turned into a crossing of agony for her, though she did not make a sound. Each lurch of the wagon over the rocky bottom sapped her strength. So, after a nap, her day passed much the same as the day before, but no visits from Nathan as he spent the rest of the day riding scout.

It wasn't until they stopped for the night and he came to help her down so she could relieve herself that she got her chance to talk to him. Jessica was wrapped snuggly in a blanket. Once her feet touched the ground, she forced herself to straighten then wobbled as the pain took her breath.

"Easy, just breathe. Sara will be here shortly." Nathan

steadied her while the dizziness passed.

"I'm fine." She pulled herself away.

He eyed her. "Sure you are. Maybe I should carry you."

"No," she jerked up her head then gasped at the sudden movement. Nathan stepped back to her again.

"I didn't mean to—"

There were tears in her eyes when he looked down at her. "You're too independent of a little thing."

Jessica could not take her eyes from his and was not sure if the new loss of breath was from her ribs, which she almost forgot about, or the way he said 'little thing'. It was almost a caress. No, she was being foolish. She pulled herself in check and remembered she was going to ask him about her money belt.

She glanced around to make sure no one was in hearing distance or paying them overt attention. "Mr. Hawke, I must ask you while we're alone about my money belt. Please tell me it's safe."

"It is."

"Please, I must … I would feel better having it back."

"It's safe," he repeated.

"But I would feel safer to have it with me."

"You can't wear it right now."

"The wrap on my ribs is higher." She broke off at the shake of his head.

"You can't wear it. The thing is bulky. It might have worked to protect you earlier, but it would pain you now."

"You don't understand. It has all I have. It's a lot of money. I don't want to risk it being stolen."

"I don't think anyone would steal it."

෮෨

Nathan started to wave it off, wondering just how much she could have then paused, he hadn't looked. He'd been too upset finding out that she was a woman, and she was asleep when he'd stowed it in the wagon.

96

"I will make sure it's safe." He could see she wanted to argue, but the sight of Sara coming their way ended the conversation, forcing him again to wonder just how much she did have. Twenty, maybe forty or fifty dollars, it was possible. The belt had been heavy.

He watched the two women move off, Sara keeping Jessica at a slow pace. Just how much was she carrying? Unable to stand the curiosity, he climbed into the wagon and pulled the belt from where he'd stuffed it almost negligently when he'd returned two nights ago to get his belongings before going to Jessica's bedroll. Not that he'd slept he remembered.

He tested its weight feeling how heavy it was before laying the money belt on his lap. He untied the leather bindings and pulled out three leather envelopes. When he opened the first his heart almost stopped in shock. By the time he got to the third, his anger was back. The weight of the pouch, which he presumed was full of silver dollars, was mostly ten and twenty dollar gold pieces. The little fool was carrying what most would call a fortune strapped to her body.

Seven hundred and sixty-eight dollars, he forced air into his lungs. What was she thinking? No wonder she was concerned. She should be panicked. He could have stolen it from her, and no one would have believed it.

Now he did have to find somewhere safe for it. He thought of fastening it to his body, but there was always a chance of getting hurt and someone taking it just like what happened with her. He moved some things around until he came to the tools he had packed away that he wouldn't need until he started to work on his new home. He placed the money belt in the bottom of the box, covered it with large nails, repacked the box, securing it and burying it at the bottom of the wagon. Next, he straightened out her bed back over it.

Looking down, he figured it was about as safe as he

could make it. He climbed back out of the wagon in time to see the women coming toward him. Jessica seemed to move with more ease, though her steps were measured, not her usual quick paced actions from before. As she drew nearer, he noticed the pallor, which had disappeared earlier, had returned. Without a word, he helped her into the wagon, deciding he could discuss the money later.

Nathan finished tending the horses. Mrs. Garfield brought him some dinner for which he was immensely grateful. After eating he decided it was time to speak to Jessica. He was trying to think of her by that name now. He liked it.

At the back of the wagon, he paused to take a deep breath to steel up his resolve, but when he lifted back the flap, he saw her eyes closed. Lowering the flap back down, he shook his head and sighed. Once again, she had avoided his lecture.

When he settled in Jess' bedroll underneath the wagon for the third night, sleep again was delayed in coming. He thought of the woman who slept above him. It was impossible not to think of her. He found it both disturbing and comforting to think of her.

It was comforting having the things that he kept sensing about her confirmed, but it was disturbing just the same. He felt a pull to her he could not deny. Not like the contentment he had when he had chosen his wife, but more like he was standing in the middle of a field with a lightning storm flashing all around. The power of it almost shocked him. Then what shocked him more was that he had thought of Jessica in the same thought he had of his late-wife.

It was all wrong. What he felt for Jessica was anger. No. He had given up lying to himself years ago. So he decided not to look any closer at what Jessica raised in him, except maybe a protectiveness because she was alone and scared, well, maybe not scared, but hurt. There was no way he was going to think on it more.

"Right," he shifted in her bedroll and was greeted with the scent of her. *That was enough of that, he needed some sleep.* Eyes closed, he forced his mind to clear.

Nathan wasn't quite sure what had disturbed him when he popped awake. There were no unusual night sounds. One of the horses shifted in the grass but no hint of danger. He looked out and studied the stars that he could see around the scattered clouds. It was well past midnight, he judged. There was still time for a few more hours of sleep. He was just drifting off again when the small cry reached his ears.

Jessica, his mind came back alert. When the cry was followed by another he scrambled from the bed. His pants were on because he had worn them to bed. He didn't bother with his boots or pause to think before he climbed into the back of the wagon.

The interior was dark, but there was enough light to make out the outline of the woman who struggled in the bed. "No," she cried then gasped. "No." Her hands batted out at nothing and Nathan felt himself relax. She cried again then whimpered with pain.

"Jessica." Nathan crawled forward and leaned down. "Shh, Jessica it's all right."

"No." She struck out with her hand and he barely got his own up to catch it before it contacted with his cheek.

"Jessica, its Nathan."

"No, don't, don't." She tugged on her arm, swinging out with her other hand. Nathan caught that one too, but it only seemed to set her off. "Jessica, please, you're all right. Your horses are all right. They're safe."

She jerked, cried out in pain and gasped for a breath. Nathan debated on releasing her and slipping out of the wagon, but her next cry was so laced with terror he couldn't. "Jessica, wake up." He winced at how demanding and harsh it sounded, but it seemed to do the trick. She stilled then her eyes fluttered then opened.

"That's it." His voice softened on its own accord. "Now you're with me."

"Nathan?" His name was a question that was followed by a flood of tears.

It was her trembling with the tears that did him in. "Shh now," he lowered himself down then lifted her enough to slide his arms around her. "It was just a dream."

"He was, he was," she repeated then cried against his shoulder. "I hate him. I wish it would go away."

Nathan got a sick feeling in his stomach as his mind worked to put things together. Jessica was fleeing something, obvious choice, a man. Was it a husband? Could she be married? Of course she could. She was of the age and was pretty enough to be sought after by a great number of men.

He didn't want to think that she might have an abusive husband. What had she said about her stepfather? Was it all a story or was there truth in it? She said he made things difficult to stay. If the horses were hers and something in him did not let him doubt that. What would cause her to flee her home?

Another wave of sickness hit him. He knew there were cases where a stepfather or step-brother would turn their attention to a younger female of the home who no longer had protection. And again, Jessica was pretty enough to draw attention. He didn't want to think of it.

He ran his hand down the back of her head. She was still now, and he realized she had fallen back to sleep. He started to lower her down but she whimpered and clung to him tighter, he froze. After a few minutes, he tried again only to receive the same reaction.

At a loss as what to do, he shifted enough to lean back against a bundle in the corner. He would leave the minute she settled into a peaceful sleep. Her scent teased his mind. It was the same fragrance of the past that stirred him, but now smelling it up close it was even more enticing. It felt only right to turn his head and draw in her fragrance. It was a nice smell. It was Jessica, he thought as he drifted off to sleep.

The sound of footsteps near the wagon filtered into Nathan's mind pulling him from sleep. He became aware of the scent and weight of Jessica pressed against him about the same time. He realized it was the second time it had happened, but this time there was not any feeling of wrongness. Still, it was almost as disturbing to him as it had been when he thought he had been attracted to a boy. He stayed a moment longer enjoying the feel of her against him. There was no denying it felt very good.

Again, he heard the sound like someone not far from the wagon. Alert this time, he listened and decided he'd better check it out. Besides, it wouldn't be good to be caught in there alone with Jessica. Her reputation would be at stake, and he had already encroached on propriety once already.

He detached himself from her in small cautious movements, but it paid off when she settled back into the down mattress with only a sigh. He slid over the edge of the wagon then decided to check on the horses once more before turning in.

"Up late?" The voice of Emory Hayes startled him. He hadn't seen the man in the darkness.

"Just checking on things."

"Took you a mighty long time to check on the girl, noticed your bedroll empty a while ago."

"She had a nightmare."

"And you comforted her good, I bet." The sneer was clear in the man's voice.

Nathan could feel his ire rise, but didn't jump to the bait. "Just sat with her until she went back to sleep."

The man snorted, "Knew we'd be slowed up by her. I say we best get rid of her fast. Even though she might have a few uses."

Again Nathan didn't take the bait. "That will be decided when she's well enough."

Hayes snorted again then turned and went off.

The wave of unease he experienced was not the first one given him from Hayes. The man was crude and he didn't trust him.

Chapter Ten

Jessica felt better the next morning when she woke. Her body was still sore, but at least she no longer felt like she was going to faint each time she shifted. Figuring she could make it out on her own today, she wrapped the blanket around her, pushed back the canvas, and stepped over the edge.

"You will not stay still, will you?" Nathan's words startled her. She slipped off the step only to be lifted into the air as an iron firm arm caught her beneath her knees and another slid behind her back. Jessica found herself held in midair for a minute. It was a dizzying effect being held against Nathan Hawke's chest. The man was unnerving to her senses.

"If you'd waited just a few minutes more Sara Hammond would be here to help you."

"I'm much better today."

"I seem to remember you tried to convince me of that yesterday."

"I am better. I feel much stronger. I want to get dressed and check on my horses."

"Your horses are fine. I've already tended them. If you'd like to step around the end of the wagon to the left, you can see them. As for getting dressed, I believe Sara was going to see about finding you something."

"I told her not to bother. I have my own."

"And I believe I made it clear the other day you would not be using those clothes again."

"I have my own dresses, and there's nothing wrong

with my old clothes."

"Not if you're a fifteen year old boy, but you're not. How old are you anyway?"

"I'm," Jessica paused, she had forgotten about the date. "What day is it?"

"It's the twentieth."

"The twentieth really, I'm eighteen. That means no one has any say over me. I'm free." The feeling of elation that washed over her was so strong it was like a burst of power. The Meadows was hers, the wealth was hers. No longer did she have to fear Raker or her stepfather because they could no longer force her into a marriage she didn't want.

"I take it you just had a birthday."

"Yes, I did. Two days ago."

"Well, it wasn't a very good birthday, I'm sorry."

"There's no reason to be sorry."

"Then back to your attire."

"I have my own dresses," she cut in. "They're in the bundle with five half-hitches on the top."

"All right, while you go with Sara to clean up, I'll move it into the wagon. Then if you feel like dressing, you may before we pull out," he turned to move away.

Jessica remembered she was going to ask again about her money belt. "Nathan," she reached out and caught his forearm.

His eyes came back to her with a deep penetrating feel, and Jessica lost her train of thought.

"Maybe we better move back to Mr. Hawke. It would be more proper." His words brought a wave of pain that snapped her free.

"Mr. Hawke." The words tasted sour in her month. She cleared her throat and continued. "I wanted to ask you again about my," she glanced around and dropped her voice, "money belt."

Jessica could have sworn anger flared in his eyes.

"It's as safe as I can make it," he growled out. "What

do you think you're doing packing that much money around on your body? Do you know how much you have?"

"Yes, to the penny."

"There are men out here who would kill you for less than a tenth of what you have," he paused, "or a single horse."

"I understand that." She felt hurt by his obvious low opinion of her. "I did make a plan. I thought being disguised as a boy I'd attract less attention."

"On a wagon train, without a wagon."

"I don't need a wagon, but I decided it would be safer to travel with the wagons than on my own."

"Now we get to the truth of why you disguised yourself. So you could get on the train."

"Yes."

He reached out and touched the edge of her hair. "Did you cut your hair?"

"Yes."

"Was it long?"

"Yes."

"I like the look of it still, but I would have liked to have seen it long."

"It will grow. It actually grows quite fast."

"Jessica, you're up, good. I hope you haven't been waiting long." Sara's voice cut off any further discussion.

"Morning, Sara," Nathan said and moved off.

⊗≈⊗

She was just eighteen. He was almost seven years her senior. Well actually it was less than six and a half, but he felt much older. She seemed young and innocent. His thoughts went to her nightmare, and he wondered what she had been through. It had to be something awful to give her such lingering terror. He didn't want to think of a man hurting her. She should be loved and cherished.

He shook the thought away and went to retrieve her clothes. It wasn't hard to find the right one. She had used

ALYSIA S. KNIGHT

the knot combination to mark them. The bundles were heavy, and he wondered again what she carried. He was tempted to look inside, but didn't have the right. She had a lot of belongings, especially for someone who was running away. He just hoped it wasn't from a husband.

❧

The bundle on the mattress was the first thing Jessica noticed when she climbed back in the wagon. Nathan had removed the knots so she wouldn't have to struggle with them, but it looked like he hadn't opened it. She was so busy contemplating the meaning behind it, she didn't notice Sara follow her in.

"Good, Nathan fetched the bundle. Shall we find you something to wear? That is if you still feel up to it."

Jessica nodded and moved forward to pull back the oil-cloth.

"Oh, what a pretty night gown," Sara exclaimed. "You were certainly right. You definitely don't need to borrow anything from Olivia. That girl will be livid that she is no longer the best dressed female in the camp."

Jessica grinned at the older woman, and picked out one of her favorites to wear for her first appearance as a woman. After dressing, Jessica was worn out and the pain was once more taking her breath, though she felt better now that she was dressed.

"There," Sara said from behind her. "Won't you surprise them. There will be no more mistaking you for a boy now. Who would have thought? You fill out that dress quite nicely. Why don't you get some rest though before you come out?"

As much as Jessica wanted to object, she just didn't have the strength. "I think I will."

"I'll just leave this bread and mush for you."

Jessica must have dozed off because it was the voices of men talking outside the wagon that disturbed her.

"Now that the girl is up, about, and on the mend, we

106

need to be deciding what to do about her." The voice was so muffled she couldn't make out who it was.

"It's simple. Just marry her off." Jessica thought that might be Mr. Sanders.

"We only have two unmarried males who are old enough to take a wife. And I honestly would hate to see any girl forced to marry Hayes. Not to talk down at the man, but even though the girl was deceiving us, she seems nice enough and is a hard worker."

"That still leaves Nathan."

"But a man like Nathan could have any woman he wants. Why would he want a slip of a thing that looks more like a boy than a girl?"

"The girl is right fine with horses just like him."

"True enough. Still, I don't know if he'd be interested, but there's no doubting that Hayes could be persuaded. Those horses of hers make a right fine dowry."

The men moved off leaving Jessica feeling sick inside. There was no way she would ever marry Emory Hayes. Never! She would leave the wagon train first. She would just wait as long as she could, until she was stronger.

Now that she was thinking more clearly, she knew she was still too weak to make it on her own. Just shifting the packs to get her dress out wore her out. But she was also now certain her ribs weren't broken, just badly bruised, and they were getting better.

A few more days and she'd be able to boost the packs onto the horses again and she'd leave. She had made it on her own before. Her disguise had worked. The trail was easy to follow. She had plenty of supplies.

It was noon rest-stop when Jessica made her way out of the wagon. After steadying herself, she made her way to her horses.

⟪⟫

The cool water had felt blessedly good to Nathan. The days were getting warmer. He should've changed to his lighter undergarments, but when he thought of it, Jessica had been in the wagon. He would have to start thinking ahead. He'd gotten out of practice of thinking about a woman's sensibilities.

He gave his hair a final rub with the toweling as he approached the camp then froze catching sight of a woman by the horses. Her head was blocked by Lady's head. He blinked trying to bring who it might be to mind but was unsuccessful.

The body was lithe, trim but more curved then Olivia Freeman's, unless the girl was adding padding which he figured was possible. It still couldn't be her. This woman was taller, and Olivia Freeman would never be with horses voluntarily.

Nathan changed his direction and headed for the horses. He was still a good fifty feet away when the woman came around from behind the horse, rubbing its nose and talking to it. Nathan stopped again, petrified as his mind tried to digest what he was seeing, and make it fit his preconceived notion. It just didn't work, though the short hair on the woman confirmed it could only be Jessica Wells.

There was no mistaking her for a boy or a girl. She was a woman, a very attractive woman. Nathan didn't realize he was walking toward her. One of the other horses moved over and butted her arm for attention. She staggered slightly and grimaced but turned to greet the horse.

"You should be careful. He could hurt you."

She looked at him obviously startled. "Jasper won't hurt me."

"Not intentionally, but he's young. He doesn't always know his own strength. You're in no condition to get butted by his head."

"I'm doing much better, and he's just missed seeing me. I don't think there's a day before now that he hasn't seen me."

"I understand that," he took a final step toward her. Like the horse, he seemed to need to get closer to her. "You look nice in a dress."

"You sound surprised."

"I'm not actually. I just wondered. Even with short hair, you look nice.

"I've been afraid to look in a mirror."

"Don't worry. You look good, but there's a little bruise right here." He touched a finger to her cheek.

She lowered her head, and he could have sworn she blushed.

"It was foolish getting hurt. I was just thinking about the horses," she said softly.

"I can understand that. I would have probably reacted similarly."

"But you would have caught them. Do you think they'll be back?" There was a pleading look in her eyes when she lifted her head.

"No, they know we're alerted now. It would be stupid of them. Try not to worry. If they did try, they wouldn't get close."

"You sound sure."

"Titan got a good scent of them when they tried to take him. They spooked him. He won't let them near again. If they try, he'll make enough of a ruckus to draw attention." He followed her gaze over to Titan.

"He covered Lady." There wasn't a question in her statement.

"Yes, she's okay, I checked her over," he assured her.

"I guess that I owe you a stud fee then."

"We don't know for sure yet."

Jessica shook her head. "I don't doubt him."

"I could always take the foal off you."

"No, Titan's a beautiful horse. I'd like the foal, and I'm willing to pay the stud fee. I had already decided to talk to you about it. I'm not sure when Misty or Rose will be ready, and we probably will not be anywhere close to you when it comes time for the foal to be born or old enough to be weaned."

"It sounded like we're headed to a similar area in California. That is, if what you told me as Jess is the truth." There was a touch of bite in his voice.

"It was," she answered defensively.

"So you're running off to be with the horse trainer?"

"It's not like you're making it sound. Amos is older."

"Older than your father?" He wondered if she was looking for a father figure.

"More like the age my grandfather would have been. He was there when my father was a young boy. He's in his sixties."

Nathan could tell she was getting defensive, but couldn't help prying. "So if you're not running to him, who are you running from?"

"Who said I was running?"

He remained silent for a moment and watched as she shifted.

"You mentioned before your stepfather was making it difficult for you. Was that true?"

He didn't think she was going to answer when she surprised him with a weak, "Yes. My stepfather didn't like the idea he couldn't get control of the property and money that went with it. My father was careful in making out a will that protected it for me to receive one day."

"What did he do to you to make you run?"

"It doesn't matter. He will not get The Meadows." She looked away, not meeting his eyes.

"It does matter." He raised his hand to touch her arm, but stopped himself. "He hurt you enough that you have nightmares."

"That was not about my stepfather."

"Then who hurt you?"

"I said it doesn't matter. They can't reach me now."

"Because you disguised yourself as a boy and ran off."
He shifted closer to her.

"I did what I had to do. I will continue to do what I
have to do."

"You could ask for help." He moved forward another
step.

"And who am I supposed to ask? I tried to join two
different wagon-trains as a woman and was turned away.
They would not even consider letting me go, but if I were a
male, even one too young to be out on my own, or a lazy,
no good one, I could go as long as I was a man."

Fire blazed in her eyes as she looked at him. "Mr.
Hawke, I can make it on my own. I don't need charity from
you or anyone else. I do appreciate what you've done for
me the last couple days. I will pay you for your help and
inconvenience. I will also pay you the stud fee. I believe
forty should be more than fair compensation."

Nathan stood, amazed at her. It would have been truly
spectacular if her body didn't weave with fatigue. Her
bluster was spoiled again when she must have realized he
had her money. The look that crossed her face was
precious.

"If you will please retrieve my money belt, I'll pay you
and be out of your wagon and way."

"What would please me is to have you lay down before
you fall down." And with that, he took that last step
dividing them and scooped her into his arms before she
could protest.

"Mr. Hawke," she squeaked.

"You will be quiet and not argue or I will double the
stud fee."

"Mister–"

He cut her off again. "Not a word and you're not
paying me for helping you. That's because it's what people
should do. Since you seem to need a lesson in that, we will
start now. I will carry you back to the wagon so you won't

fall and mess up that pretty dress that you look so nice in, in case I didn't tell you. You will then say thank you and lie down and rest. The lead wagons are already moving, so get settled. After a rest, if you want to move up to the seat for a while, you can join Joseph Hammond there. I'll be riding scout this afternoon. Please don't give the boy a hard time. He will already be stunned at the sight of you in a dress."

Nathan suppressed a groan as he lifted her up into the back of the wagon. What he couldn't say was if it was from the strain or the feel of her pressed against him as he tilted her over the tailgate. He didn't give himself time to debate. The moment she touched the mattress, he released her like she was a hot coal, feeling singed.

Chapter Eleven

Jessica was still sitting in the same position when she heard Titan burst from where he'd been waiting for his rider. She fumed, not sure what to make out of what had just happened. Nathan Hawke was an infuriating man. He had been kind, almost chivalrous until he turned prying, then went right to bossy.

She was tempted to show him by climbing out of the wagon. Before she could, the wagon jerked and pain flared in her side. They were in full motion by the time the pain subsided taking with it her strength.

Nearly two hours passed before she woke and crawled out on the seat next to Joseph. The thirteen-year-old almost dropped the reins when he whipped his head around to get a second look at her. His jaw fell open as he stared.

"Afternoon, Joseph," Jessica tried not to laugh at the boy's reaction. "Mind if I sit out with you awhile."

The boy managed to smile and shake his head.

"Thank you. I'm getting tired of being in the wagon. It's nice out here but a little warm." Something in the boy's reaction was gratifying along with maddening. What was so shocking of her in a dress anyway?

Jessica worked at talking to him like normal, and he finally relaxed and responded to her as usual, though every once in a while she caught him taking a furtive look when he thought she wasn't looking.

Nathan managed to get Jessica out of his mind after a tiring race across the meadow. He scouted out the area ahead locating an excellent place for the evening camp and had just started making his way back when he came across a young buck and brought the deer down, saving the need of a hunting party being sent out later.

The wagons were parallel from his position when he finished cleaning and loading up the deer. They were only a short ways from where he'd marked an area for the evening camp when he caught up to them. His wagon was bringing up the rear as usual but, what wasn't normal was the sight of a woman on the bench. He knew it was Jessica though a bonnet covered her short hair. She looked good there.

Nathan could hear them talking as he came up behind. "I'll take the reins if you want to go join your family."

"I'm not sure if that's a good idea. You could hurt yourself."

"Nathan's team is good. They won't pull on me,"

"But if you get hurt—"

Nathan picked that moment to interrupt. "I'll tell you what. I'll take over the reins Joseph. You can take Titan and this deer up to let everyone know that we have fresh meat for tonight and let your father know not to send anyone out. Then you can bring me a nice piece back for our dinner."

"I can do that, Mr. Hawke." The boy handed the reins to Jessica, jumped down and Nathan took his place.

"Are you having a nice ride, Miss Wells?"

"Yes, thank you, Mr. Hawke. It feels good to be out."

"You're not over doing it I hope."

"I've just been sitting here," she answered sharply.

He got the point that she was still upset with him for his high handedness. They fell into a companionable silence broken by only brief touches of conversation, but he was fully aware of her at his side.

Nathan had started a fire and was watering the horses when Joseph arrived with the meat. Jessica was the one to greet him. "Joseph, this is wonderful. Can you move the

Dutch oven over to the fire for me?" she asked.

"Should you be fixin' dinner?"

"I can handle this. There'll be no need to move it around before Nathan comes back from watering the horses." She watched as he thought about it for a moment.

"I guess that'll be all right if you're sure you won't have to move it."

"I'm sure. I'm just going to add some fixin's to it and make some skillet cornbread, and there's no lifting there."

Joseph seemed satisfied and left after settling the oven over where some good coals were forming.

While it was heating, Jessica busied herself retrieving her seasonings from her packs and some of her precious vegetables. She'd just placed the meat in the oven when she became aware of someone behind her. Instinct told her it was Nathan, and a quick glance over her shoulder confirmed it. He was staring at her with an odd expression she couldn't quite figure out. She'd say there was fire in his eyes, but she hadn't done anything to make him angry.

"You're fixing dinner?"

"I owe you one for helping with the colt. I never did that, and besides, it's the least I can do with everything you've done for me – letting me stay in your wagon, tending my horses and packs. Cooking meals is something I can do. Though it will in no way repay what's owed."

"I said you didn't have to repay me. But, I won't complain having you fix some meals. I thought, after the first time I had your cooking we should have gotten together and shared the chore, but I figured you wouldn't be happy with the trade because I'm only a passable fair cook."

"I don't mind cooking. Actually, I enjoy it."

"Good. Is there anything that I can do to help?"

"I'm doing fine. It's almost all prepared, just cooking time. If you have something you need to do, I'll call you when it's ready."

"If you're certain?"

"Yes, it will be some time still."

"All right, I'll be close if you need me." At her nod, he left.

With the cornbread in the pan, it would only be a short time for dinner to be done. She turned to see Nathan leading the last of the horses back from the creek. Making a quick decision, she headed toward him.

"May I join you?"

"Come away, most are your horses."

"I know, but I didn't want to intrude. You seem to have developed a ... rhythm.

"You won't bother me. In fact, if you feel up to it, why don't you do a light brush down on the ladies and I'll start on the gents."

She smiled as she stepped to get the curry and brush before moving to Slippers.

"Just don't overdo it," he cautioned as he brushed down the powerful hind quarters of one of the big pulling team. "You start to get tired or hurt, you stop."

"I will, I promise."

"Good."

She started to run her hand over the pregnant mare. "How are you my sweetie? Getting close? You're holding up good." Without thinking, she started singing.

"They missed you. Now I know why they don't settle down the same for me. Do you always sing to them?"

"Usually, but if people are around, I usually keep it soft so not to be heard."

"I heard you when the colt was born. I thought you sounded like a girl."

Jessica was ready for his ire to rise like it always did when he came back to her deception, but this time no anger came.

"I'm like the horses. I like your singing."

Jessica felt the warmth rise in her cheeks and turned

her head. "It's just like your talking to them. You pick up a melodious tone that is very soothing."

"We're both good with horses."

"Yes, I'm better with horses than people I'm afraid." She reached up and rubbed the mares ear.

"I don't think so. You get along with Jon."

She laughed. "He's impossible not to get along with."

"Not quite so. A lot of people say he's a pest."

"Not at all, he's just curious."

"You know, the morning after we found out you were a woman, the men were talking about it. They were shocked and couldn't believe it. Jon was standing in the middle of the group by his father and right out loud turned to his father and said, 'What are they talking about? Of course, Jess is a girl, what else would she be? I don't think you ever had him fooled."

Jessica shook her head smiling. "I wondered a couple times but it didn't seem to matter, and I didn't know how to broach the subject with him, so let it be."

She moved to the next horse and fell silent for a moment before picking up the conversation again. "I believe Slippers is getting close to her time to foal."

"Yes, I've been keeping an eye on her."

"Thank you. Do you think she will have problems like Ruby?"

"No."

"I feel better with you here."

"I'll be handy but odds are she will be just fine."

"I hope so. I'm not ready for another like Ruby's."

She finished and went on to the next horse. Her movements were slow and cautious compared to Nathan's. His were motion quick and fluid. He was doing two horses to her one. When she finished the horse she was brushing, she cleared her throat. "I think I'd better go check on dinner so the cornbread doesn't burn."

"Cornbread, that sounds good. I'll be there as soon as I

finish and wash up. Don't try lifting the oven out of the fire. If you need it out before I get there, just call."

She nodded, accepting his counsel, knowing it would have started an argument and she really didn't want to argue with Nathan. Not when the last half hour had passed so pleasantly. A quick wash up and check on dinner proved it was about done.

Jessica prepared to remove plates and utensils from her packs then remembered she saw the ones in Nathan's wagon and decided his would be easier to get to. Dishes in hand, she stepped back out of the wagon turned and nearly dropped the dishes.

Emory Hays stood two feet behind her, his shirt was marked with sweat and dirt, but what was fouler was the way his eyes scanned her body. It was the same sickening look that Clifford Raker used to look at her with. "Who would have thought that a scrawny boy could fill the front of that dress out so well?"

Jessica was so shocked at his words she couldn't respond. She was taken farther back when he took a step toward her. "If I let you sleep in my wagon, will you fix me supper?" He leaned down so that rancid breath wafted over her face. "I'm willing to come join you in the wagon also now I know you have some—"

"Hayes." Nathan's voice sharply cut off whatever the man would say next.

Hayes looked at him. Jessica saw Hayes's eyes flash with hatred then he smirked, turned and walked away.

Jessica didn't move until Nathan took Hayes place in front of her and said her name softly.

She hardly managed to swallow the lump in her throat. "I don't like how he looked at me." Jessica got the feeling Nathan agreed with her, but he didn't say it.

"Ignore Hayes. Are we ready for dinner? I'm washed up."

"It's ready if you'd like to move the oven from the

coals."

"My pleasure," he shifted it then removed the lid. "That smells good."

They were finishing up when Joseph came up with another large piece of meat. "My pa sent this over for tomorrow. Ma suggested that Jessica, Miss Wells, might be willing to fix it for the Sunday potluck."

"Potluck, tomorrow's Sunday?"

Jessica turned to Nathan for confirmation.

"Yes." He seemed hesitant to answer her.

"Can you fix it?" Joseph asked, clearly confused.

Nathan answered for her. "Yes, of course. I'll give her a hand."

"Good. Nathan, my father told me to tell you that he wanted to talk to you tonight if you could stop by."

"That's fine. I'll be by in a bit."

The boy nodded and left.

"Jessica."

She knew Nathan was talking to her, but was having trouble focusing on him. All she could think of was what Sara said about them waiting to decide what to do about her until camp council on Sunday, and that was tomorrow.

Her mind replayed the conversation she'd overheard. She would have to marry to stay, and there were only two unmarried men, Emory Hayes and Nathan Hawke. Nathan wasn't interested in getting married again or he would be. He could have any woman he wanted. That left Hayes. At the thought of Emory Hayes a wave of sickness hit her. There was no way. She would have to leave tonight even if she wasn't ready physically. She'd just have to do it.

"Jessica." She jerked up her head as Nathan touched her arm. "You over did it. I'm a fool for letting you up yet."

"I'm all right," she managed to get out.

"You've gone deathly pale. You better lie down. I'll clean up."

"I'll help."

"No, you won't. It was a wonderful meal, but it's my time to help with it. Now in the wagon," he turned her to the wagon, and Jessica decided not to protest as he helped her in. If she was leaving some rest would be good, still she was surprised when she actually fell asleep. She woke with the sound of voices.

"Sorry Jacob, I was planning on coming over in a minute. I had to clean up and do a few other things first."

"Where is Miss Wells?"

"She's sleeping."

"You're certain?"

"I checked on her a minute ago."

"Good, it's her who I wanted to talk to you about. Tomorrow we have the council and need to decide what to do about her."

"Don't you think it's too soon?"

"She is up and about and it needs to be done. The consensus I've been getting is she can stay if she gets married. And as one of the two unmarried men in the camp, I wanted to know your thoughts on the matter."

There was a moment of silence. "I understand the rule of no single females, but I can't say I'm in favor of her being forced to marry. I think that it's wrong. I wouldn't like to be forced into a marriage."

There was another silence. "Emory's willing to marry her."

"You can't seriously think of forcing a young woman to marry someone like him. Hayes is on his last warning before being forced to leave. And marriage is for life. Jessica doesn't even like the man, and I can't blame her. I don't like him either. He's vermin, a lazy drunk."

"I agree, but there aren't many options, the only one being is if we can talk everyone into letting her stay with us to the next fort. Maybe she can find someone to her liking there. Either that or she'll have to stay there. It's a sure bet Hayes will vote for marriage though I know a couple who will agree with you, and I'm against making her marry him."

"Are you saying it could go either way?"

"I am."

"And what about her?"

Jessica waited for the answer, but if it came, she never heard it.

That was it. She was leaving – running again. She was not going to marry Emory Hayes. She'd make it to California on her own. A shiver ran through her that she knew was fear.

"Please, Father in Heaven, please help me," she prayed with her whole heart. Her money-belt, the thought hit her, and she started to search, wincing when she moved several boxes. Wherever Nathan hid it, she couldn't find it. She gave up with the thought that maybe he had strapped it to his body. It made her sick, but she'd have to leave it. There was no choice. At least she had her supplies, and if she could locate Nathan in California, he'd return the money. Her heart jumped at the thought of seeing him in the future.

Jessica lay still until long after the camp grew quiet. She heard Nathan climb into the bedroll under the wagon and realized he'd been using hers which meant she'd have to leave it but that couldn't be helped and she had other quilts, if she could get her packs. It was going to be tricky with Nathan here.

She waited late into the night to be certain he was asleep and whoever was on night watch would be tired before she started to work her way from the wagon. She froze and waited at each of the seemingly thousands of creaks that sounded. The stretch from the wagon to the ground sent a burning in her side but she could handle it.

Her packs were piled along one side of the wagon to give Nathan a wind break if needed. It would be hard to get them, but at least her cooking one was a little off to the side from when she used it for dinner.

She would get that one then collect what else was possible. When she moved the pack and could see the empty bedroll, she almost fainted with relief. Nathan was on watch. The noise she heard earlier was just him laying out the bedroll. This made it easier and more difficult. She could get to her belongings, but Nathan was more alert on watch then some of the others.

A small gasp escaped when she lifted the first pack. After the second, she realized she couldn't take them all. She was sweating from pain by the time she got the third moved to the horses. She would have to sacrifice what wasn't absolutely essential. Luckily, the most necessary items were packed together.

Her next decision tore at her more. She'd have to leave the pregnant Slippers with Nathan. Riding hard on her own wouldn't be good for the mare. It would also be best leaving Ruby and Coal, the colt being so young.

Nathan would need two of the other horses to bring the packs she was leaving. At least, she hoped he would bring them, maybe if she gave him Slipper's foal and paid him for his troubles. That meant she'd have to leave a note and let him know she would locate him when he got to California.

She released Jasper off the line and moved him into the shadow close to the tree where her saddle was propped. One of the other horse's whinnied and he answered back.

"Shh." She stroked his neck a second before reaching for the saddle. Taking a deep breath, she hoisted it to her chest, which screamed with pain.

Lights swam in front of her eyes. She staggered but held on and forced it up higher to the horse's back. Dropping it down, she sagged against Jasper pressing her cheek against the smooth leather. Tears streamed from her eyes and her body shook.

"What do you think you're doing? I could have shot you as a horse thief if you hadn't been wearing the dress."

Nathan's voice was low and menacing.

Jessica couldn't raise her head to look at him, embarrassed by the tears, and the fact that she hadn't got her breath back and was still too dizzy to move.

Chapter Twelve

Nathan moved around the camp thankful it was his turn for watch. He was too restless and needed to move. Something was wrong and he had no doubt what it was. Thoughts of Jessica being forced to wed Emory Hayes burned in him.

She would never do it. This meant, once they got to the fort, they would leave her there, and she would be forced to marry someone passing through to move on and pray they were better than Hayes. Well, most any man would be better than Hayes, but he hated the thought of her with some other man who might abuse her. Her nightmare still burned in his gut.

He was on the circle going toward his wagon when he saw a figure among the horses. Hand on his gun, he moved forward. The men were fools to try for the horses a second time, especially after hurting Jessica. He covered the distance before he realized how small the figure was and that it was wearing a dress.

He saw her lift the saddle and fury leap within him. That was it! He was going to tan her hide. Watching her slump against the horse did nothing to calm his anger.

"What do you think you're doing? I could have shot you." He stepped forward. "I mean it Jessica." One more step and he grab her shoulder and turned her, then shoved the gun in her face for proof.

Moonlight glistened off her tear streaked face. Under his fingers he could feel her trembling. "You hurt yourself," he bit out, shoving his gun back into the holster before pulling her gently to him.

"I need to … catch … my breath." She sagged against him.

He wanted to ring her neck, but when his hand found its way there, his fingers wouldn't tighten past a caress. He felt her breaths deepen as she took air into her body. Nathan slid his fingers up through the soft silky ends of her hair, taking in the scent of her and had to force his mind back to what was happening.

"Where do you think you were going?" he growled out. "No, don't answer, let me guess. You were running away."

She shook her head against his shoulder. "Running away refers to belonging. I don't belong here."

"Do not attempt to argue that."

"I will not marry Emory Hayes. If I wanted to marry someone like that, I would have stayed home."

"It will not come to that. I won't vote for it."

"But you can't stop others."

"I carry a lot of clout."

"I know you do, but your word is not final."

"No, it's not, but you can't make it out there on your own. You can hardly get the saddle on the horse."

"I will be better in a couple days, and I'd already decided to leave some of the horses with you. I'm willing to give you Slipper's foal in exchange for their care."

Nathan felt a wave of shock that she'd consider leaving her horses with him and even more that she would give him one. They were precious to her. "You'd trust me with your horses? Trust me with this, stay here. Wait for the decision then, if you have to run, you can, but give yourself another day to heal." He knew his argument was weak, but he had her exhaustion and pain to sway her. "One more day, after council tomorrow you can still leave."

He knew he had won when she sagged deeper against him. It was hard to get past the thought that Jessica had really been going to leave. It terrified him. She must have heard him and Jacob talking. If he hadn't caught her, she'd be gone.

He didn't want to picture her out on the trail alone, but the image came all too clear, followed by one of finding her body along the way. She'd be a lot safer if she didn't have so much spirit. But would she be as intriguing? There was no answer to that.

When a sigh slipped from her and she rubbed her cheek against his chest, he realized she was more asleep than awake. There was only a slight sound of protest when he lifted her then she snuggled against him. Nathan looked to the horse waiting patiently for his rider. "I'll be back in a moment to put you to bed, boy. First I must see to your mistress."

A second later, he decided he was getting pretty good at getting into the wagon with her in his arms. By the time he got Jasper resettled for the night, it was time to wake his relief.

A few minutes later, he stretched out on the bedroll. Jessica Wells was once again playing havoc with his sleep, yet now he wondered what he was going to do if the men wouldn't give on the subject of an unmarried woman in the company. There was no doubt now that Jessica would go it on her own. He couldn't let that happen. He just wasn't sure what he could do to stop it.

☙❧

The bright morning sun was cutting through the wagon pulling Jessica from sleep when Sara pushed back the canvas. "Good morning. I didn't see you out so I decided to come check."

"I guess I overslept."

"A little, the camp council is already going on."

At the word council, Jessica shot up, a hand going to her side as it protested with pain. "It's that late?"

"Yes, you must have been exhausted. You fell asleep

in your clothes."

"Oh no, I need something else to wear. Can you get me my pack?"

"Actually, it looks like Nathan left it for you."

Jessica turned to see it at the head of the wagon. "Oh."

"I'll help you change then we can sneak over and eavesdrop on the men."

Jessica would have smiled at Sara's comment if she wasn't so worried about what was happening. She picked one of her better dresses.

"Oh, that is beautiful and smart," Sara exclaimed. "Attack them with feminine innocence if the meeting is not going in your favor."

"Do you think it will work?"

"Well, it probably won't hurt. I know Jacob was concerned about it. It's such a sticking point. He's on your side. That was agreed if he wanted to stay on my good side. Let's go see what we can overhear while I get you some breakfast."

"Thank you."

The woman made a shooing motion with her hand. "It's nothing, Jacob would tell you, I'm a born busy body and it came to me directly from my mother who, if anything, is worse."

Jessica sat on the back side of the Hammond wagon so she could hear and go unnoticed.

"Rules were set and established before we left. It's the same with all the other companies. She knew she was breaking the rules, or she would never have dressed like a man in the first place." She heard one of the men.

"We have two eligible males here, and one has already volunteered to marry her so there's no problem," Mr. Richmond pointed out.

"There is a problem not giving her a say on who she's going to marry." The voice was loud and clear, and Jessica recognized it as Nathan's voice, her heart jumped.

"She had all the choices she wanted in finding a husband before she tried to come." She could not place that voice.

"We don't know that. We don't know the circumstances which she came from." It was Nathan again.

"That's all here or there. It doesn't matter." Jessica finally placed the voice of Mr. Freeman.

"That's right. I'm willing to take her." Jessica shuddered at Hayes's comment.

"Would anyone of you men that are fathers want that for your daughter?" Nathan shot back.

"Nathan has a point there. I wouldn't want my daughter forced into a marriage like this. I couldn't abide by it."

"That's my husband," Sara whispered. "I knew he'd listen to reason."

"My daughter would never have run off on her own. It is totally unseemly. The girl is fortunate to find a man still willing to marry her after such questionable behavior."

Jessica sucked in a breath. She'd like to show Mr. Freeman 'questionable behavior' by walking out there and punching him in the mouth. How could he say something like that when Olivia was such an obvious flirt?

There was a grumbling among the men that Jessica couldn't figure out if it was good or bad, but she felt sick again when Emory Hayes spoke back up.

"Freeman's right. We don't know about her chastity after all, being out on her own. We do know Hawke has been back in that wagon with her alone several times. She could be a fallen woman for all I know."

"Now wait a minute," Mr. Freeman objected. "That was not what I was suggesting."

"But it's true," Hayes said forcefully.

"I can assure you nothing has happened when I've been in with her. She was injured." There was rage in Nathan voice.

"So you say, but she spent the night in your wagon on another occasion that we all know of when she wasn't hurt. How is it you didn't say anything about her being a woman then."

"Because I didn't know, she stayed fully dressed."

"In wet clothes? It was raining that night." Hayes' tone went past suggestive to accusation.

"She had changed before I got there."

Hayes grumbled something Jessica couldn't hear then spoke up. "I know her virtue is questionable, but I'm still willing to take her. It's hard for a man to get a woman out west. From what I've heard, a man can't be too choosy about certain things. And I guess those horses of hers make a decent enough dowry to overlook a few flaws."

It was hard to believe that Hayes could be so well spoken, the snake. She had all she could take when Nathan spoke up again cutting off the grumbling.

"Wait a minute, since there's a question that I have … purged Miss Wells' honor, then, if she is to marry someone, it should be me."

Jessica felt as if her heart stopped.

"I thought you weren't willing Nathan?" Jacob Hammond spoke up.

"Be quiet man," Sara said behind her.

"I'm not willing to see her forced into marriage, but if she is going to be, I want her to have a choice in the matter."

"And you know she'd will be willin' to take you over me." Hayes moved into her view, the man's bulging chest was puffed out. "I agreed to take her first."

"Yes, but Miss Jessica will have a choice. She can choose you, me, or neither. In which case, I will break from the company to escort her to the nearest fort. She can stay there, find someone and then I'll go on."

The uproar echoed across the clearing.

Jessica still couldn't believe what she heard. Nathan

would leave the wagon train for her. She couldn't let him do that. They needed him.

Jessica moved without thought from behind the wagon. Head held high, back straight, she walked into the middle of the men. The group fell silent as she crossed to where Nathan stood.

"Mr. Hawke." She raised her chin a little higher so she could look him in the eye. "I have come to ask, if you would be willing to marry me?"

Chapter Thirteen

Nathan was still taking in the vision of Jessica walking toward the group. She was glorious. The sun caught the yellow of her dress, making her like a beam of light. When she moved, hips swaying so smoothly in her determined stride, his pulse leapt. His pulse jumped again when he heard her ask him to marry her. At that moment he knew that was exactly what he wanted. It had been there the moment he found out she was a woman, or at least after his anger had settled.

"It would be my pleasure if you would marry me?" Meeting her eyes, he returned, needing to ask her the question.

"Yes sir, I would be honored to marry you." Her answer was stiffer and more formal than he wished, but they were hardly in a setting that allowed for a heart filled declaration.

"That's settled then," Mr. Garfield, a big barrel-chested man, bellowed out. "We can have the wedding after services and a feast and dancing to celebrate.

"Perfect." Sara Hammond stepped out and clapped her hands to her bosom. "I'll get the ladies preparing the feast."

ೞೲ

Jessica didn't hear a word of the service. She was mortified. How could she have just marched up to Nathan Hawke in the middle of everyone and asked him to marry her? She couldn't stop trembling. What was she thinking? What would she have done if he'd said no?

Heavens, what was she going to do? He'd agreed. He

was marrying her because he had promised to help her. It wasn't that he wanted to marry her. He was being noble.

She never should've asked him, but when he announced he would marry her after standing up for her so, her heart just leapt like some silly, twittering girl over a hero. Now all she wanted to do was cry. She had trapped Nathan into marriage.

He was now in as bad a situation as she had been. The only difference was that she really wouldn't mind being married to Nathan. A wave of fear rippled over her at admitting it to herself. She was attracted to Nathan Hawke like she had never been attracted to any other man before. But, could she force him to marry her and be stuck with her the rest of his life? If she didn't marry him, she would have to leave, and honestly, though she was willing to do it if she had to, the thought frightened her.

The solution hit, leaving her feeling hollow and sick inside, but she knew she would have to do it. She needed to find Nathan as soon as services were over. The wait was interminable, but it gave her time to figure out details. After the prayer was finished Jessica tried to reach him, but she was quickly surrounded by a group of women all bursting with excitement.

Jessica finally caught up with Nathan back at his wagon where he was stoking the fire. "I thought we better check on the meat. It's fine."

"Yes." She moved closer. "Mr. Hawke."

"I think, all things considered, you can call me Nathan again."

"Oh, yes, Nathan. I wanted to apologize to you."

His head came up and he stared at her. "Apologize?"

She fidgeted. "Yes, I put you on the spot back there. It was not fair of me, but I do have a solution," she added hurriedly.

"A solution," he repeated her again.

"Yes, a marriage of convenience. Then when we get to

California, we can get an annulment and you can go on your way. I'm willing to compensate you for your time and effort."

"Compensate, why is it you're always trying to pay me."

"I'm only trying to be ..." She recoiled at the temper that rolled off of him. "I will not force you into a marriage you don't want."

"Who says I don't want it?"

"If you wanted it you would have suggested it earlier. But this will work. We can travel together. I will do the cooking and help share the chores. I will try not to be a problem, though I do realize, that for the next few days, I won't be much help still, but I'll help where I can, cooking, laundry. I will really try not to be in the way."

ଓ୨୦

Nathan wasn't sure how to react. He had just gotten the idea of being married to her settled in his mind, and now she was talking a marriage of convenience. He saw nothing convenient about it.

He wondered what she would say if he said that. What would she say if he told her, he wanted her married to him in every sense of the word? Obviously though, that was not what she wanted. What was he to say? That he wanted all rights that a marriage to her would give him. No, he couldn't force himself on her.

"If you are certain that is how you want it."

She nodded at him though he thought she looked about to cry.

He managed to move his head up and down in a nod. "I think it would be best to keep this arrangement to ourselves."

"Yes, I agree." Her hands smoothed over her skirt several times before she locked them together in nervous reaction. "Well, I guess I should get some seasoning for the meat if you'll shift the oven for me."

Nathan watched her walk off feeling oddly bereft. Not that he had been planning on a honeymoon tonight. Jessica was far from healed enough for that. Still, he liked the idea of being able to sleep beside her. Maybe even hold her, though there was no doubt the sweet fragrance of her would drive him crazy. Now there would be no way to sleep beside her and know she would never be his. That was too much to ask of himself.

Nathan was surprised at the number of seasonings that Jessica possessed. He didn't know what most were, but liked what it did to the meat. "There's no reason for you to pack the spices. The spice box is about empty. Besides salt and pepper, I didn't buy much. I'll make room to add any of the cooking utensils you want out and your clothing. I have room, and there are things I won't need to get into that can go into your packs if we need room."

"There's not much I need out, just some clothes, and they are in the packs you moved in already. Most of the other items are from my trousseau or that were mine from my grandmother, and I didn't want to leave them. It was probably foolish of me."

"But you wanted them." He understood. He too had brought items that had been in his family.

"Yes."

"Are there any packs you'd like me to put in now?" He could see her hesitate. "Which would you like?"

"The one with six hitches."

"I'll get it for you."

With the meat cooking, Jessica finally had free time. She guessed she should be getting ready for her wedding. She eyed the bundle Nathan had left by the wagon before he went down to the river.

She thought of the formal gown she had packed away. The silk material in the palest blue, trimmed with wide white lace would befit a wedding dress, but this really wasn't a true wedding. Then again, it was likely to be the only wedding she would get. The dress was way too formal for a wedding on the trail, but it was too formal for anywhere she would be in the future.

"You look quite lost in thought." Sara drew her attention.

"Oh, yes."

"I thought you would be running around trying to get yourself prettied up. Not that you're not beautiful now, but I figured you'd want to go down and bathe and wash your hair."

"I would like to do that."

The woman nodded. "I don't think anyone has any finer dress than what you're wearing, so it will do well."

Jessica looked back to the bundle.

"Jessica," the woman said her name as if it wasn't the first time she'd said it and Jessica made up her mind. "I actually have another dress if you would help me with it."

"Of course."

The woman waited while Jessica opened the oil cloth and then the canvas. "Isn't that a lovely quilt?"

"My grandmother made it for me." Jessica fingered it a moment, wondering if her grandmother would approve of what she was doing. She thought she might. She moved the quilt aside to reveal the gown.

"Oh my, that's the loveliest thing I've ever seen. Of course you must wear it. Oh what a beautiful bride you'll make. Nathan will be drooling for the wedding night." The woman paused. "I guess he'll have to wait for that until you're better. What a shame. Still it's good for a man to learn patience and in time …"

The sentence was left hanging, but Jessica knew there was no finishing because there would be no wedding night for her and Nathan.

An hour later Jessica had bathed and washed her hair. Sara had pressed the wrinkles out of the gown and was lacing up the back.

"You don't need that corset to fit the dress, but it will probably help protect your ribs. We should have thought of it before."

"I don't like to wear them. I didn't pack any others."

"Well it's nice you packed this one. You know that lace shawl makes a prefect veil. It's crocheted with such a fine thread.

"My grandmother again."

"Well, let's see how it looks." Sara laid it over her hair then fussed a little with her bangs.

"I have a couple of combs." Jessica got out a smaller bundle and unwrapped it.

"Those will be perfect along with the choker with the ring of light blue sapphires on the silk band."

"What do you think?" Jessica asked once it was tied in place.

"You're so beautiful. The men will be so envious of Nathan and the women will be envious of you for that gown and marrying Nathan. He's a good man. You're very fortunate."

"I would be if I thought he wanted to be married to me."

"Hush now child. Don't you ever think that Nathan doesn't want to marry you. No one could make that man do something he didn't want to do."

"No, he's doing what his honor dictates him to do. Sara, he is a good man, an honorable man. He knew I didn't like Hayes, and he stopped me from leaving."

"You were going to leave, out here in the middle of nowhere? You wouldn't have done such a foolish thing." The woman paused. "No, you would have. I'm so glad Nathan was there to stop you. And, I still say, he is marrying you because he wants to, but I guess it will take time for you to believe that. There's one thing for sure, when he sees you, he'll be counting himself very fortunate."

"I just hope he doesn't regret it."

"He won't."

Jessica wished she could be as positive as the woman.

"Now, it's time to head over." They were halfway there when Jon came running toward them.

"Hey Jess, you look nice in a dress."

"Hello, Jon."

"I brought you some flowers. Hannah said you were supposed to have a bouquet of flowers and be told you look nice."

Jessica started to laugh as she accepted the bouquet of Buttercups and blue Jonny Jump-ups. The flowers were perfect coming from the boy.

"Thank you. Did you come to escort me there?"

"I just came to walk with you. I'm glad you're marrying Mr. Hawke. You both like horses." The boy studied her. "Though, you can't ride in that dress, he will still think you look pretty.

"You're right. This is a dress for parties, not riding horses."

"Everyone is all gathered over there so we can eat and have a party after. Everyone is all dressed up fancy." He looked to his mother. "I had to keep my church clothes clean."

"You did a very good job of it. Now, why don't you run and tell your father we're here?"

"Yes, Mama." He disappeared around a wagon, and Sara pulled Jessica back to a stop.

"Just wait up a second. You want to make an entrance. Let me look at you. Perfect." The older woman said after a moment. "Smile, you look lovely."

"Thank you." Jessica leaned forward and brushed her cheek against Sara's giving her a hug. "Thank you for everything."

"You're welcome. Now stand tall. How are your ribs fair'n? Good?"

When Jessica nodded, she continued. "Good, give me a moment to get settled, then make your entrance."

A wave of nervousness hit Jessica as soon as Sara vanished. Butterflies tumbling inside her. She placed a hand over her stomach, drew in a deep breath and tried to still her heart. The tightness in the corset made a deep breath difficult, but Sara was right. It did help her ribs. Managing several smaller breaths, she counted to twenty before she stepped around the wagon.

ᏨᎳ

Nathan felt oddly nervous as he talked to Jacob Hammond. He was getting married again. The thought was strange to adjust to, but what was really hard to accept was the 'in name only,' a marriage of convenience.

He should have set Jessica straight and told her he wanted a full complete marriage with her. But what if she backed out and ran? He couldn't risk that. So it was a marriage of convenience.

Jon came running up. "Mama said to tell you they were here."

With that, Jacob raised his hand motioning to everyone and the crowd fell silent. Sara came waltzing in.

"Jessica has on a dress and looks very pretty. She smells nice too, but she can't ride a horse in her dress. It's for parties. So she won't wear it all the time and will be able to ride again later," Jon announced.

"Thank you for letting me know that." Nathan leaned down to speak to the boy who nodded and moved off to his mother. Nathan straightened in time to feel his heart lurch. The woman that appeared from behind the wagon wasn't just pretty, she was beautiful, a vision. Each time he looked at her she seemed to get lovelier, but there was no out doing this.

For a time in his life, he had moved in circles of formally dressed women, but few could hold a candle to Jessica. Her waist was so slim he'd swear he could span it with his hands, yet she wasn't overly thin. In fact, she was very nicely curved. Her eyes shown bright as she glided toward him.

Desire hit him stronger than ever. There was nothing convenient about this marriage of convenience. Each step she took toward him, the more certain he was that he was meeting his destiny. There was no doubt in him he had to win her.

She looked nervous but that was understandable.

When she raised her eyes to his, they locked there. She gasped before her lips curved into a smile. Heavens, she was breathtaking. He reached out a hand for her as she drew near. She took it. Her fingers trembled as he drew her close.

"Are you all right?"

"Yes, my heart is pounding. I'm nervous."

He gave her fingers a squeeze. "It will be fine, trust me."

"I do," she said softly with great confidence that warmed his heart.

"Save that phase for in a few minutes." He could have sworn her smile brightened at his words.

"I'm practicing."

"It sounded good to me."

"If we're ready to start," Mr. Richmond stepped forward. "By the authority granted to me as a designated minister for this wagon train and witnessed by this company we are here to join this man and woman."

Nathan lost track of what the man was saying when he looked down at Jessica's face. Her eyes were bright with unshed tears. He studied her face. She had such fine features. No wonder she always kept her hat so low. If he could have gotten a good look at her, there would have been no doubting she was a female.

Her nose was slightly sharp, lips bow shaped with the bottom lip on the full side, made for kissing.

"Do, state your full name please."

"Nathanial James Hawke."

"Take, state your full name."

"Jessica Alethea Wellington."

Nathan wondered if his eyebrows rose like Richmond's did, but he continued. "I do." Nathan knew positively when the words come out, he meant it.

A moment later relief rushed over him as he heard Jessica say 'I do' without even a quiver as she looked to him and smiled.

"Then by the authority given to me, I pronounce you husband and wife before God and these people." Mr. Richmond leaned in. "You are allowed to kiss her now."

"Oh, yes," Nathan whispered just loud enough that Jessica must have heard it because she looked shocked. "There are some pleasures in life a man just gets to do," he said as he leaned forward so only she could hear.

"You want to kiss me?"

"I do. Nice phrase."

She let out an "oh" just as he claimed her lips. Her lips were soft and gave to him as he drew her in. She was perfect in his arms. For a moment, he took her in then carefully eased her back. Her eyes were still bright but there were no tears in them now. She did seem to be trying to catch her breath, and Nathan felt a wave of satisfaction.

⟨⟨⟩⟩

Jessica wasn't sure what happened, but it felt as if her world had been tipped upside down. It wasn't like that when Raker had kissed her, but then, she hadn't wanted him to kiss her.

Was this what it was like when you were interested in a man? Did she really want Nathan to kiss her? With how she was feeling, the answer was a definite 'yes', and she wanted him to kiss her again. Before she could catch her balance and lean back into him, they were surrounded.

Chapter Fourteen

Everyone came forward to congratulate the couple then food was gathered up for the feast. Jessica settled next to Nathan with a loaded plate in front of her, feeling too nervous to eat. She was aware of every movement that Nathan made.

When Nathan reached for the brisket his arm brushed her side and she nearly jumped out of her seat. Unfortunately, the trunk they were sitting on as the honored couple left no room to shift away. After a dozen brushes, she finally got used to the contact and started to relax.

"Tired?"

She jumped again but this time it was due to his breath on her ear when he leaned down to whisper to her. "A little, but I'm doing fine."

"You're not eating."

"Nervous, I guess."

"That's understandable. You've taken a huge risk tying yourself to me."

"I don't see that as a risk. I feel quite comfortable about that. I have watched how you handle your horses, you're not mean-spirited. You're a hard worker, always doing your share and more. You're quick to help others. That speaks well of you."

"I'm flattered you think so highly of me."

"I really do, Nathan," she almost tripped over his name. "I think you're a very honorable man. It makes me feel bad I have trapped you in this situation, but not bad enough for me to release you from it."

"There's no reason for you to feel bad. I wouldn't have gone through with the marriage if I didn't want to."

"I tell myself that, but I hope you're not disappointed with the arrangement."

"I'm not."

"You haven't had long enough to know."

"I think I have. Eat now, your body needs food to heal. Here try this," he picked up some meat with his fork and held it out for her. She eyed the fork a second then leaned forward to let him place it in her mouth. It was the most forward thing she had ever done and felt giddy for it.

The meat was delectable, and he seemed pleased that she'd accepted it. His eyes traced the movement of her tongue when she ran it over her lip to pick up traces of juice. Her breath caught at the intensity in his eyes, and his masculine scent filled her senses. She knew her face was turning red and looked away.

"You make a very tasty brisket."

"Thank you, but all I did was put some seasonings on it and then put it in the oven."

"It's the seasoning that makes it special. Look how everyone is enjoying it. Why do you think it was sent over for you to cook? They learned that, even when they thought you were a boy, you were a good cook. You're generous with your seasonings."

"I brought plenty, too much probably, more than I will surely use in two years. I bought spices and seasonings in each of the towns where I picked up supplies, not realizing how much I really had until I put it all together."

"Well, I am a happy recipient of your excess." He smiled at her, and then winked, leaving her completely flustered.

Jessica hadn't realized she had been eating until she looked down and found her plate nearly empty.

Nathan leaned into her. "Don't look so shocked, you're doing better."

"I feel better."

"Good, that way you won't faint on me when we dance."

"Dance?"

"Of course, we get the first dance."

"I haven't danced for a long time."

"Do you like to dance?"

"Yes, I do. I was just getting old enough to attend the dances when my father died, then my mother remarried, and Clifford wouldn't allow house parties or us to attend them. I should have known something was wrong when ..." she broke off and a shiver ran through her.

"What?"

"It's nothing. I don't want to think of it."

She could tell he wanted to press it further and was glad when he let it drop. When Sara asked a question, she turned her attention to the woman.

Jessica looked around the group. Only two people didn't look happy. Olivia Freeman's eyes were shooting arrows, and not the cupid type arrows of love, but her look was nothing compared to Emory Hayes. When Jessica caught his glare, a shiver of fear ran down her back. Fury burned in his eyes with terrifying clarity.

Jessica focused her attention on what was being said near her, joining into the conversation until Mr. Ford pulled out his fiddle and Mr. Anderson his guitar. With the music beginning, the crowd turned all their attention to the newlyweds, calling for the dance. Nathan answered with a flourish. He bowed in a big sweeping movement and extended his hand.

"Would you do me the honor?"

Jessica felt her cheeks flush again as she placed her hand in his. "I would be pleased to."

Nathan led her to the center of the group. Jessica went into his arms as the music started. His hold on her was so light she couldn't feel it though her corset, but the heat of his skin through his shirt was enough to bring another flush to her cheeks. She could feel the cords of muscle flex as he shifted her and her stomach tightened.

"I'm not hurting you, am I?"

"What?" She tilted her chin up to meet his concerned look.

"Am I holding you too tight?"

"No. You're a wonderful dancer."

"My mother insisted I learn, but I must say I enjoy it, especially with such a lovely, graceful partner."

Once their dance was over, the music became lively. It always amazed Jessica, how after a week of wearying travel, when the music started everyone seemed to be rejuvenated. Whooping and hollering filled the air with the lively beat of the dance. It took only one dance for Jessica to realize she was not recovered enough yet for much more.

Nathan walked her back to her seat and started to settle by her. "No," she shooed him away. "Go dance. There are a lot of ladies that depend on you to partner them."

"It wouldn't be right to leave you alone."

"It's perfectly all right. You can save a later dance for me in case they do another slow one."

"I'll make sure they do."

After a few minutes of watching, Jessica decided to sneak away to refresh herself. Careful not to disturb anyone she made her way around the wagons. She was surprised when Olivia appeared in front of her. The girl waited and for a moment Jessica debated on changing her direction, but it seemed inevitable that they had to meet, and there was no way she was going to run from Olivia Freeman.

"Olivia." She nodded her head in greeting.

"I hope you're happy," the girl snapped back. "You got Nathan to marry you." The girl looked her up and down. "Though how he managed to force himself to as hideous as you look in that dress with that hair is impossible to figure. You should have stayed in your boy clothing, they fit you

TRAIL TO HER HEART

better. Well, you might have got him to marry because he compromised you, but you will not make him happy. He could never be happy with someone like you. He needs a woman that knows how to be a woman."

That said, the girl turned and flounced off without giving her a chance to say a word. Not that Jessica could get anything past the lump in her throat. She knew the girl was just being catty but it was so close to her own thoughts it hurt. Her ribs burned as she took a series of rapid breaths, holding back the tears that welled inside. Jessica got herself back under control only to look up and find Hayes watching her from a wagon over.

For a moment a smirk replaced anger on his face. "Think you did better with him? You just might come to regret what you did," the man grumbled out and like Olivia turned to leave, but there was no flounce in his heavy steps.

⋘⋙

Nathan noticed the moment Jessica disappeared. After finishing out the dance, he went after her, but he didn't have to go far. She stood just on the other side of the wagons. The stillness in her alarmed him. He covered the ground in long strides, reaching out, he touch her arm. The scream that escaped her as she jumped was enough to frighten him.

"Sorry."

"Nathan," she sagged in relief, and he was only too happy to slide his arm around her waist and draw her close. "We wore you out." He liked the feel when she leaned against him.

"Just a little."

He was surprised she admitted it and realized she must be truly tired.

"Actually I'm fine, I just needed a breath and to step into the trees." She seemed hesitant. "Would you mind waiting for me?"

"Not at all, I'll take the time to check on the horses."

If she minded that he kept his arm around her as they walked, she didn't mention it. When they reached his wagon, she turned to him. "I'll only be a minute."

Nathan watched her disappear around a tree and wondered what had upset her. Jessica was hard to figure out. True, he hadn't much time to think about it yet but for all her spirit, there was a definite gentleness about her.

They made it back to the dancing for a few more songs, but Nathan decided to stay by Jessica, and she seemed content to have him there. She no longer pulled back when he brushed against her. In fact, she now seemed to lean into him a little. He lowered his head to her, "I'll be right back."

When he came back he held out his hand. "A last dance."

Once again, the music was slow and Nathan took her in his arms. For the first moment, she remained what was considered a proper distance but as he tightened his hold, she moved closer. He squeezed her fingers and she looked up.

"Did you have a nice day, Mrs. Hawke?"

"Mrs. Hawke, I hadn't thought. I'm going to have to get used to that."

"How long did it take you to get used to Jess Wells?"

"Not long, my father and Amos both used to call me Jess, and Wells is just shortening Wellington so it wasn't hard to react when I was called that."

"Do you think you can get used to being Jessica Hawke?"

"Jessica Hawke. It's kind of different but I think I like it."

"I like it too." He moved a little closer, and after a minute, her head dropped to his shoulder. He definitely liked it when she did that.

The music ended, she lifted her head and blinked adorably.

"Shall we thank our musicians and say goodnight?" He wasn't thinking how it would sound when he announced, 'He needed to get Jessica in bed'. A wave of chuckles and giggles went through the crowd, though everyone knew there could be no honeymoon tonight.

"I'll clean up the Dutch oven and bring it by in the morning," Sara volunteered giving Jessica a kiss on the cheek.

Nathan offered her his arm, and they made their way to their wagon. "Did you have a good time?"

"Yes, yes I did. I feel more accepted now."

"I think you are. People are getting a chance to know you. As Jess, you kept your distance from everyone."

"It was necessary."

"I understand."

"I enjoyed dancing with you."

"I enjoyed it too. We make good partners."

She nodded and smiled. Nathan put his free hand over hers. "I think you better head right into bed. You've been up a long time today."

"I slept in."

"Still you better turn in." Then he looked at her and paused. "You're not going to be able to get in the wagon in that dress. How did you ever get out?"

"Sara hung some sheets out for me to change behind out here."

"That's a good idea. It won't take me long."

"That's not necessary. I can change in the wagon if you'll just help me in."

"I was thinking earlier that I'm getting quite good at putting you in. If you're ready?"

"I was just thinking that you could boost me."

He scooped her up in his arms. "I like this way. There sure is a lot of dress, but you look very pretty in it. I'm pleased you were willing to go to the effort. Especially when I know you're still not feeling the best."

"A wedding should be treated special."

Nathan tightened his hold. "I agree, but I wondered if you did, where you're not thinking of it being permanent."

"It could be the only wedding I ever get. No one knows how life will go."

"That's true. You know at first, after I discovered you were a woman and after your nightmare, I wondered if you were running from an abusive husband."

"No."

"And you said it was not your stepfather."

"Partially yes it is, but he wasn't abusive to me. He didn't dare. Everything is mine, held in trust."

"So you said before. Then why are you running?"

"On my birthday, I would have come of age, and everything would have come to me as my father stipulated. My stepfather came up with a plan of marrying me off to a neighbor who would allow him to control Wellington Meadows if he could have me."

"So you ran to avoid marriage and ended up married to me." Sullenness was heavy in his voice.

"You are nothing like Clifford Raker. He and Emory Hayes are more cut of the same cloth. Are your arms getting tired yet?"

"I guess I should put you down." He lowered her over the tailgate. "Have a good night." He shifted and caught hold of the bed roll.

"Nathan?"

He looked back at her. "You didn't think I was going to sleep here."

"But it's your wagon, and we're married now. No one will say a thing if you sleep in here." Her eyes were wide, full of innocence. He knew she didn't get it.

"Jessica, it was you that suggested a marriage of convenience. If I sleep beside you, that's not going to work. You've been around horses enough to know that you can only tease a stallion with a filly so long and not expect him to do something about it. Men have needs, although we are able to control them more. We have only so much restraint, and if I start sleeping beside you every night, I will either go insane with desire or something will happen between us." He looked serious.

"I'm sorry to shock you with such plain speaking, but you have to know, if you want this to stay a marriage of convenience, there has to be a distance between us. More than there was today. For now it's not so much an issue because you are still injured, but soon that will not be the case and then, if the distance hasn't remained it will not be easy to keep it from happening. I'm sure you realize you are a very beautiful and desirable woman. If I ever touch you, the marriage will not be annulled. If I ever touch you, you will be my wife for the rest of our lives. Think about that."

With a quick jerk, Nathan pulled the bedroll over the tailgate and yanked the flap free with his other hand letting it fall, cutting her from his view. Unfortunately, it didn't wipe the memory of her looking so lovely in the pool of light blue silk. She was innocence and temptation in one. It was going to be a long way to California.

Jessica sat staring at the canvas. In the last week, she had spent quite a bit of time doing that, but this time she was trying to figure out what Nathan had meant. Did he find her desirable? Was it possible he would be favorable to a true marriage to her in every sense of the word?

A rush of excitement ran through her until her mind came back to a poignant part, he did not say anything about love. He might find her desirable, but Raker had wanted her also, and there was no love in Raker's desire for her. Raker's had been rancid and ugly. And though Nathan's was not, it didn't mean it was love. She was not innocent enough to believe that. The question was, could Nathan come to love her, because after today, she was certain of one thing, she was in love with Nathanial James Hawke.

She contemplated the fact for a few minutes more until her eyelids drooped. Jerking her head back up, she realized she still needed to change. She was not going to sleep in her dress again, especially this gown. From now on, she would think of it as her wedding dress.

Pain rippled through her side as she shifted to reach the first button. After a minute of fumbling, it came free. She went on to the next. By the time she had managed the first four, she was exhausted and trembling. There was no way she would be able to do what she figured were eighteen to twenty more.

Deciding it might be easier if she worked from the bottom up, she went to work at her waist. It was easier to reach and she managed six more before it became impossible to go on. Even if she had full mobility without her ribs hurting, she couldn't get out of the dress on her own, and she didn't think she could make it out of the wagon to get to Sara. Besides Sara would be busy settling her family to bed.

Outside the wagon, she heard Nathan shifting stuff around. If it would have been their real wedding night, she could ask him to undo them. But if it was her real wedding night he would be in there with her.

She leaned back against the side and groaned. What was she going to do? She couldn't ask Nathan. That was clear by what he'd said. Besides he was a man, even if he was her husband by name, she had never been in a state of undress with a man before. Except when she was injured, and Sara had finished helping her then. He had seen her in a nightgown on several occasions, but she'd also been covered by a blanket, and this was different, he would have to help her undress down to her chemise.

No, there was no way she could do that. She'd just have to do it herself. She managed three more buttons with tears flowing down her cheeks before she gave up.

Chapter Fifteen

Nathan had thought Jessica had gone to sleep when he heard a groan come from the wagon. Silence followed, and he figured she must have been doing it in her sleep. Then he heard shifting and more gasps of pain. Nightmare, the thought hit him, and he headed for her.

When the sound stopped so did he. He waited, listening, debating on pulling back the canvas to check on her, but the vision of her was too clear in his mind. Halfway back to the fire he heard what was obviously more gasps of pain. Unable to stand it, he headed back to the wagon pushing aside the canvas without pause. He wasn't prepared to see Jessica sitting there dressed or when she turned to look at him with a tear streaked face.

"I can't undo the buttons." More tears streamed down her cheeks.

"How did you get into it?" The stupidity of the question hit him before he finished it.

"Sara helped."

Nathan felt himself sinking as the ramification hit home. He was the only one there. No, it couldn't happen. That was going way too far. The Lord would not test him so, and it couldn't be a sign because there was no way to follow through with her still in pain. What was he to do?

"Can you help me?"

He wanted to turn her down, say he just couldn't do it. It was asking too much. But he put his foot on the step and swung his leg over the back. Heat radiated up through him when she turned her back to him.

He was in more trouble than he thought. Nearly twenty of the tiniest buttons he had ever seen ran down her back. At her waist a space hung open a ways revealing her undergarments, but it was the gap at the top that showed the nape of her neck that was more disturbing. She had a beautiful neck, and it was right there as an offering to his lips. If he just leaned forward he could taste her.

"No," he said firmly to himself, she was not his.

"What?" She sat unmoving, facing forward, waiting.

"Nothing." With great effort of will he raised his hands. His fingers were awkward, and he was sweating by the time he finished the first button. By the third, he was ready to take out his knife and slice them away. By the eighth, he was ready to rip them apart with his bare hands.

The luscious column of her neck and bare skin disappeared under the linen chemise that was so fine he could see right through it and feel her heat radiating up his fingertips. A wave of desire hit him so strong it was all he could do not to clamp his hands on her arms and hold her while he ran his lips over her neck and shoulders. She was his wife, and he wanted her.

As the last button came free, he scrambled back unable to take his eyes from her nicely curved back. "You're done," he wasn't sure if he was talking about her dress or his self-control. He fell more than climbed out of the wagon, forcing a breath of fresh air into his lungs to wipe out the scent of her. It did no good. He headed for the stream and prayed the water would feel colder than it had been earlier, but he was afraid that even ice would not chill his desire.

ം

Jessica managed to make it into her nightgown, but as she lay back in bed, sleep would not come. She could swear she could still feel Nathan's hands on her back. His breath caressing her nape, and there was no getting away from his scent that surrounded her.

152

Her heart raced and she knew it was desire. She wanted him to continue to touch her, caress her, to kiss her. She wanted him to love her, to teach her how to love him. As much as she had wanted to turn to him, it wouldn't be hard to love him. He'd just have to show her what was right.

It wasn't going to happen though. He'd left the camp. She knew that for certain. There had been none of the usual quietness in his movements. He sounded like he fled the hounds of hell in his leaving. He had fled from her. Tears again stung her eyes, but these were of sorrow for a husband who couldn't stand her presence but had married her because he was honorable.

CRND

Six days. He had been married to Jessica for six days and he was already at the end of his limits. He studied the heavy thunder clouds that sat over the western mountains and decided that they were a co-extension of how he felt. His insides churned and rumbled in much the same way the clouds did with pressure building, drawing closer; getting ready to release its fury.

He couldn't blame Jessica for his condition, if anything she had withdrawn from him just how he'd asked, though he worked around her constantly. Healing nicely, she was getting stronger every day. She no longer grimaced with movements and true to her word, she was taking over as many chores as she could do. She washed his clothes, helped with the horses and, his favorite – cooked all the meals.

She was becoming more open with the women of the company and making friends. Jon constantly showed up when he was tending the horses or to join Jessica on the bench seat, the last two days keeping her company while she drove the team, freeing him up to ride scout.

Nathan watched as his wagon was the last to pull into the area he had picked for them. He would have preferred to have made it farther in the day, but after this point, there was no shelter for quite a distance, and there were a lot of preparations to do before the coming storm.

Unfortunately, now it was time to face Jessica. She had already placed the wagon in the spot he had staked out for them and was busy lighting a fire with the wood that he had gathered and left. "How long until the storm gets here?" she asked in the way of greeting.

"An hour, maybe a little longer. It looks to be traveling fast." He moved to unhook the pulling team. After staking them down, he went to check on Slippers. All day the mare had been showing signs of labor, and with the weather changes, he wasn't surprised. It always seemed storms brought births. Nathan knew when Jessica came up behind him.

"She's close."

"Very, it will happen tonight."

"You're certain?" Her anxiety was plain.

"As I can be. She's definitely in labor now."

"What about the storm? There's no way to protect them."

"Horses foal outside in storms all the time. There is a small, mostly protected spot on the other side of the boulder there. It's too small for all the horses, but she'll fit there."

"Can I come?"

Nathan nodded. "Let me get the other horses tied down first."

"I'll help as soon as I put the leftover stew on to heat."

"Thanks, we'll need to gather more firewood and wrap it in the oil cloth for tomorrow."

"You think the storm will last?"

"It might. If it lets loose like I think, we won't be going anywhere tomorrow and we'll be glad to have dry wood."

"Most of the men seem to agree. Everyone is preparing

the same way."

The horses were skittish, hardly settling even with him talking to them or with Jessica singing. Jessica released Slippers' rope and drew her off to the side while Nathan secured the others.

"She's trembling," Jessica's voice was filled with anguish when he came for them. "I can't tell if it's labor or fear of the storm."

"Probably both. Let's get her settled in here. She'll feel better." And so would Jessica, he thought. It was going to be a difficult night. He led the pair around the boulders to the small cove he had found.

"This will be perfect. Thank you, Nathan."

"For what?"

"For finding this, I know you had to have searched."

Nathan wondered about how well she was getting to know him. How could she see something so clearly but be so oblivious to his desire for her. Then again, maybe it was obvious, and she just chose to ignore it because she didn't feel the same.

He watched her stroke the mare with her small, gloved hand. He liked her hands. When she worked, she kept them protected, so when the gloves came off, they were soft and beautiful. Dreams of them touching him, gliding over his cheek, neck, chest and shoulders haunted his night. He forced the thought away. "We have a lot to prepare. I'll come back and check on her."

There was a clear reluctance in Jessica leaving the mare, but she turned and led the way. They hurried and ate the stew and bread, then cleaned up, gathered firewood, and tended the horses. Working in tandem silence, they prepared for the coming storm.

Jessica broke the quiet when he reached for the bedroll. "What are you doing?"

"Getting–"

"No," she cut him off as she marched toward him.

"You can't sleep outside tonight. It would be foolishness."

"Jessica,"

"No, I've yielded to your wishes on your sleeping out because I understand you don't desire to sleep close to me, but you will not sleep out in a storm just to avoid me." That said, she turned and rushed away leaving Nathan stunned. She couldn't believe he slept outside because he didn't want to sleep near her. No, it was not possible that she'd misunderstood that. He had kissed her. That should have made it as clear to her as it did to him. The instant his lips tasted her she became part of him.

He let the bedroll drop. Could she really believe? Maybe it was time they had a long talk. The rumbling in the sky drew his attention. Unfortunately, now was not the time.

cs೦

Jessica darted between the rocks heading for Slippers. Out of view, she sagged back against a rock. *"Oh, Heavenly Father, now what am I going to do. I must have sounded like a love crazed fool, asking him to sleep with me. That was not what I meant though. I won't force him into a relationship when it would make him tied to me for the rest of his life. I love him too much to do that. But there is no wisdom in spending the night in the rain. It's just like before when he took me into his wagon. Can't he see, the stubborn man!"*

Jessica brushed the tears from her face, heading for the mare. "How are you doing girl?" She ran her hand down the horse's side. She felt her stomach tighten with a contraction. Jessica waited for it to pass. "Oh, that was a good one. It's not going to be long now."

The horse moved around unsettled. "I wish I had a nice dry stall for you and a bed of straw. Unfortunately, that won't happen, though like Nathan said, horses have been foaling outside for centuries. You're doing just fine." The horse shifted again and Jessica felt the sides tighten as the mare's body worked to expel the foal. With a few huffing sounds Slippers went down to her knees and the ground.

Jessica knelt beside her. "We're getting real close, aren't we?" She stroked the animal and started to sing. A few more contractions followed then Slippers threw her head up trying to look behind her.

"Easy there girl, it's almost here."

The horse lay flat with its sides heaving violently. "That's a girl, that's a girl. Nathan!" Jessica yelled without thinking.

"It's all right." A hand settled on her shoulder. "I'm here. She's fine, watch."

Jessica could do nothing else as a pair of hooves appeared. The next contraction brought long legs into view then the rest of the body came sliding free. Immediately the mare pulled up, its head going back to lick the foal. A minute later she was on her feet doing a better job of cleaning it.

Tears stung Jessica's eyes as she watched the pair.

"It looks like we have a new filly. She's a beauty. A half-sister to Coal, I'd guess."

Jessica nodded still unable to get anything passed the lump in her throat. The filly was here. They were both okay. "Aren't they beautiful?"

"They sure are. Each time I see a birth it's like witnessing a miracle."

"That's how I feel." She looked at him.

"Come here." He reached out pulling her toward him. Jessica stepped in expecting a comforting hug, but his mouth came down and caught hers. Comforting lasted only a second then it flared with heat. One arm slipped around her waist holding her. The other hand slid up the back of her neck, cradling her head while his mouth worked a miracle of its own.

Jessica lost all thought except for Nathan as she tried to follow him in the kiss. She tasted him and groaned with pleasure. She thought she heard him growl in response. His tongue slid across her lips. She gasped at the sensitivity of it, and his tongue slipped inside. The world tilted. Jessica thought she might faint and clung to Nathan for support, giving herself over to him.

The contact broke and he ran kisses over her face. She fought to catch her breath. His lips brushed hers again, but instead of settling there, he tucked her face into his neck. His hands ran up and down her back. His chest heaved as if he too struggled for breath.

"It's all right, everything will be perfect."

Jessica wasn't sure what he meant then forgot the words as his lips lightly caressed her temple.

They remained in that position until their breathing had settled and heartbeats returned closer to normal. Still reality didn't seep back in until the first drops of rain landed on their heads. Above the sky rumbled.

Nathan released her. "They seem to be doing fine. We'd better get back to the wagon before we're soaked."

Jessica studied the mare and the foal, which was up on her long legs, nursing from its mother, totally unconcerned with the black clouds overhead and the coming storm.

"They should be safe from the storm. At least they are as sheltered as we can make them." Nathan took her hand and led the way. They were almost back at camp when Nathan stopped. "Something is bothering Titan." He eyed the stallion. The horse kept moving around pawing the ground, throwing his head from side to side.

"The storm?" Jessica picked the most obvious thing.

"Must be," Nathan agreed, but didn't sound convinced. "You better get in the wagon while I get him settled."

Behind her, Titan continued to throw his head and paw the earth even as Nathan advanced. "Easy boy, easy. What's got you all stirred up? You've never been this skittish in storms before."

Jessica found his voice soothing as he talked to the

horse, but it was obvious the soothing tones that usually worked so well with the stallion, weren't helping. Jessica grabbed the last few things that had been left out and secured them under the canvas.

Turning back, she watched as Nathan stroked his hand down the stallion's neck. Even from a distance, she could see the large animal quiver. Nathan turned and made a slow study of his surroundings, looking for what could be bothering the horse.

Jessica put her foot on the wagon step to boost herself inside when a shrill whinny of a panicked horse rent the air. She dropped to the ground and spun around. It wasn't Titan. Nathan was already running from the stallion in the direction he had come a few minutes earlier.

∽∾

Nathan dodged around the boulder. At another whinny he put on more speed. He heard the snarl just before he saw the mare and foal. A mountain lion was crouched on a rock just above the horses.

Startled by his appearance, the cat's attention shifted to him. Nathan reached for his gun only to find it gone. Too late he remembered putting it away when he cleaned up from dinner, thinking there was no reason for getting it wet when they were all settled down for the night and he wasn't scheduled on watch.

He only had a moment before the lion crouched and launched itself in the air with its powerful hind legs. Nathan pulled his knife from its sheath only a split second before the cat impacted with him. He had managed to get his arm up to cover his face and throat, but there was nothing to soften the force of the weight hitting him. Man and cat tumbled to the ground. He rolled free several feet away, but the lion was on him in an instant.

Nathan drove his knife into the mountain lion as it sank its teeth into his arm, while claws dug into his side. He shoved the knife deeper. The mountain lion pulled back. It swayed as it circled him but its attention didn't waver. Nathan forced himself into a ready position for the next attack. There was nothing else he could do as he watched the cat get ready to leap.

Chapter Sixteen

Jessica started after Nathan just as she heard the animal's cry coming from the direction he'd gone. She had never heard the sound before but knew instantly that it must be a mountain lion drawn by the smell of the fresh birth. The mountain lion would be looking for a kill, and Nathan was heading right for it.

His gun, he didn't have his gun! She had seen him store it in the wagon. It took precious seconds to run back to the wagon and locate where he left it. Gun in hand; she tore off in the direction he'd gone. She heard another snarl followed by a series of groans. She skidded around the rocks in time to see the huge cat in a half crouch on one side, blood matting its fur.

Nathan was stumbling to his feet, blood coating him. He grimaced as he watched the mountain lion. The lion sprang.

Jessica raised Nathan's pistol, steadying it with both hands. The gun jerked in her hands. The mare squealed in fear. The cat kept coming, taking Nathan down. The scream caught in her throat. Afraid to shoot again in case she hit Nathan in the pile. All she could do was watch. It took a second to realize both forms were still.

"Nathan!" Jessica rushed forward keeping the gun at the ready.

The upper part of Nathan's body was blocked from view by the mass of muscle and fur. The stillness of his legs deepened her panic. *Calm down*, she ordered herself mentally, forcing her hand out to touch the mountain lion.

The big body was warm under her touch but also very dead.

"Nathan," she dropped the gun and yanked at the animal, but barely budged it as it weighed at least as much as she did. She shifted to the side to get a better angle and shoved with all her might. It slid to the side and collapsed in a heap, but Jessica paid no more attention to it. Every part of her being was focused on the man she loved, and hadn't even told yet.

Blood streaked across his face and soaked his clothes. But his chest rose and fell as he took in a breath.

"Nathan." This time her cry was soft and accompanied by tears. She stroked a hand down Nathan's cheek wiping away some of the blood. When Nathan's eyes opened, it jarred her into action. "Nathan, Nathan, can you hear me?"

She wiped more blood from his cheek. There were no cuts, so she moved down. His arm lay against his chest. She could see the tear in the sleeve and more in the side of his coat.

His arm was the easiest to reach so she started there. Gently lifting away the material, she worked her fingers in the hole and ripped the material apart.

"I expect you to fix that."

Jessica looked up, meeting his eyes. They were alert now, but she could see pain in them. "How about I just give you mine? This one is pretty much ruined."

"Or will be with you tearing it."

"Where are you hurt?"

He concentrated a minute. "Sorry, I must have hit my head when I fell. My arm throbs and my side burns. Where's the mountain lion?"

"Dead. I need to check your wounds then go get help." Jessica pushed his coat out of the way and went to work on his buttons. When she lifted the material, it revealed four three-inch long claw marks across his side, but they were not as deep as she feared. With his shirt tail, she wiped away the blood oozing from the cuts.

Nathan winced, "How bad?"

"Bad enough, but not as bad as I feared. It'll have to be stitched up."

"How's your sewing?"

"Mine?" She looked up horrified.

"Don't you think you can do it?"

"Only if I can't find someone else who can."

"That's my girl."

She managed a smile. "Let me see your arm." Again the bite marks were not as bad as they could have been. Nathan must have gotten his arm full into the back of its mouth because, instead of four deep punctures, there were a series of smaller ones. Around the area, the arm was discolored where the powerful jaws had clamped down. Without warning, Nathan raised his arm to look at it.

"Not bad, but still throbs."

"Hold still. I'm going to get some help to get you back to the wagon."

"I can make it. How's Slippers and the foal?"

For the first time Jessica thought of the horses. She looked over at the new mother. The foal was on its feet safe behind her mother. There was a fearful look in Slippers' eyes, and Jessica could tell the mare didn't like the scent of the mountain lion so close but was calmed by the two humans.

"They're both fine," she answered then her anger flared. "What do you think you were doing taking on a mountain lion? You could've been killed. No horse is worth your life. Of all the foolishness, you didn't even have your gun."

"Actually, I didn't plan on taking on a mountain lion with just a knife. It sort of happened, and I seem to remember saying something similar to you not so long ago."

"This is not a joke."

"I'm not joking. How does it feel to be on the worrying

side?"

"I'm going to hit you."

Nathan smiled at her threat. "Just wait until I'm healed."

"Nathan." What she would have said next she wasn't sure because the sound of men coming distracted her. "Over here. We're over here. Nathan's hurt." Tears again came to her eyes.

"Hey, I'm going to be alright." With his good arm, he reached out and brushed the tears away.

"Jessica, Nathan, we heard shots." The voices were coming closer. "What's going on?" The men stepped into the opening.

"Look at the size of that cat!" One of them exclaimed.

"Can you help me get Nathan back to the wagon?" Jessica called the men's attention from the animal.

"The mountain lion got him?" It was an absurd question for intelligent men, but at least they looked away from the mountain lion to see Nathan on the ground.

"Gracious," Jacob Hammond pushed past Mr. Freeman to come forward. "How bad?"

"Not bad," Nathan answered first. "I can walk but I wouldn't mind having some help getting to my feet. That'll be the awkward part. Then I'll be fine."

"You'll have some help back," Jessica put in. "Mr. Hammond, who has the most experience with sewing up wounds?"

"Sanders has had some doctor'n. Sara is a fair hand at stitch'n. Learned it from her mama and has had plenty of experience with our family and neighbors."

"Will you send someone to have them meet us at the wagon when we get there with Nathan?"

"George," he motioned to one of the men, and he moved off.

Nathan spoke up. "Can you also get someone to drag that lion away from the mare? She's had enough tonight."

"You have a new foal. The cat came for it," the man observed.

"Yes, when Nathan came to check on the horse, it attacked him."

"Jessica shot it." Nathan put in with a touch of pride in his voice.

"Looks like you got your knife in it, too." Garfield's deep voice rumbled out. "It was dead either way." He knelt by the cat. "I'll see to it. You'll get a nice hide. I'll skin it out tomorrow if the weather clears."

The weather had been totally forgotten, the overhang on the cliff above kept hardly any rain from falling in the little area. Nathan had picked a perfect spot. Just a few feet away, the rain pounded down. Above, the clouds rumbled but no lightning showed.

Jacob helped Nathan make it to his feet. Once there Nathan stood on his own.

"I'm surprised you heard the shot." Jessica hovered near Nathan, heedless of the rain.

"At first I wasn't certain, but there were too many of us that looked out to check. When you weren't at your wagon, we decided to investigate. You'd been seen going this way."

"Thank you for looking." Jessica noticed Nathan grimace and reached for him.

"I'm fine," but he caught her fingers and held them in his hand. Falling silent, they tucked their heads and hurried through the rain.

Jessica climbed in the wagon then reached to help Nathan in. She knew she wasn't much help, but he let her assist him. As she turned to light the lantern, Mr. Sanders climbed in.

"Heard you tangled with a mountain lion and won."

"Yeah, but it got in a couple licks, too."

"Let's have a look at those. Jessica, you want to help me get his coat and shirt off."

"Just cut it."

"It seems you wouldn't let me do that to yours, same goes now. I'm going to need mine still." When he started to reach for the button, she ended the teasing. "I'll do it." She was conscious of every sign of pain Nathan showed and the ones he didn't.

"Nasty," Sanders commented, leaning forward to inspect them. "I've seen a lot worse though. What we need to do is clean them out down deep before they can be sewn up, so no infection will set in. It's not going to be pleasant. It'll hurt like the devil, but I have what I need."

"I want Jessica to leave first."

"Nathan," Jessica felt a stab of pain, but it faded away when he reached out and cupped her chin in his palm, lifting her head to meet his eyes. "I don't want you to watch this, please."

There was no way she could refuse his request, but only managed to nod.

"Please stay out until Sara comes to stitch me up or, if you want, you can wait until she's finished."

Jessica knew another tear made its way down her cheek while she leaned forward to brush her lips against Nathan's own cheek an instant before she picked up her shawl and slid out of the wagon. She ignored the rain, marching back and forth, freezing when she heard him hiss then moan.

Jessica managed to hold back the wave of sickness that threatened. She didn't notice Sara had arrived until Mr. Sanders climbed out to confer a moment before assisting her up into the wagon. When she moved to follow Sara, Mr. Sanders stopped her.

"It'll be alright, Jessica. I wasn't lying when I said it wasn't too bad. I think I've cleaned it well. You should expect the possibility of a slight fever; his body has had a violent shock. Do you know how to handle a fever?"

With great effort, she managed to raise and lower her

head.

"Good. If the fever becomes too high, I want you to get me. Understand?"

"Yes, thank you."

"You're welcome. Take good care of him. Keep him warm and dry."

"I will."

Inside the wagon, Jessica tried not to cringe or gasp when Sara pulled the skin back together then put a stitch in it. "How can I help?"

The woman didn't pause. "Wash up and hold the skin together for me. It'll make it easier and less painful."

Jessica had to fight to keep from trembling as she held the tattered flesh in place. She glanced up to find Nathan watching her.

"You're handling this well."

"It would do no good to panic."

"That doesn't stop a lot from going into hysterics.

"I'll probably start shaking and crying later."

"I'll try to be ready."

Jessica knew he thought she was teasing but she wasn't. "Actually, I'm quite serious. From the time I was little, my father told me it was not good to panic when there was trouble. If I had to, save it for later when there was time. I'm not sure how, but I've always been able to do that. So when everything is all taken care of and nothing left to worry about, I will probably collapse into tears."

"I'm forewarned then."

"Yes."

"If you ask me," Sara joined the discussion, "It's an excellent way to release the stress. I do that sometimes myself. Jacob used to grump about it, but he always volunteers to hold and comfort me while I cry."

"I'll remember that as one more of those things a husband just has to do."

❦

Nathan wasn't sure how many times Jessica had reached over to run her fingertip over his forehead to check for a fever, but he was beginning to like it. It almost made getting injured worth it if he didn't feel so awful. He figured that he was feeling about like Jessica had a week earlier. His arm, side and head throbbed. If he had to pick which was worse, he'd say it was his head. He had hit it hard when he went down. The way he was feeling sick, he'd guess he had a concussion, but he wasn't going to tell Jessica. She was fussing enough.

One thing he was now certain of was that she cared for him. He was surprised when she had insisted on helping him out of his outer clothes. Her cheeks were beautifully rosy when she finished and hurried to tuck him into bed.

He drew in a deep breath and the scent of her filled him. Well, he'd be spending the night in the wagon, but not like he had hoped. The talk he planned to have with Jessica was going to have to wait until he felt better and could think clearer. He did not want to mess it up.

He heard Jessica shift something around and looked down at the end of the wagon where she had tied a quilt. Her head appeared at the corner then the quilt lowered, and he almost forgot he had just been attacked by a mountain lion.

He thought she couldn't get any more beautiful then she'd been in her wedding gown. She was a sight to behold in the white nightgown with embroidery around the neck. She was so beautiful.

When Jessica knelt at the edge of the mattress, Nathan closed his eyes and joined her in a prayer of thanks. Afterward, he peeked through lowered lashes, watching her pick up the brush and run it through her hair. He wondered if it was a nightly ritual or if she was just putting off going to bed. There was a slight tremble in her hand when she put the brush down and hesitated before moving the quilt aside. If he was uncertain about her nervousness, it was confirmed when she laid on the very edge of the bed.

"You'll be more comfortable if you'd lie flat instead of hugging the edge," he spoke up and she turned to face him.

"Nathan, I thought you were asleep."

"I was for a second."

"How are you feeling?" Her fingers brushed his forehead again.

"I'm good. I'll go back to sleep when you get settled in bed so you can sleep."

"I can sleep here."

"Then, so I can sleep." He reached for her only to stop when pain shot up his side. She was there immediately, grabbing his hand, bringing it back to his chest. Nathan managed to intertwine their fingers so her hand was pressed to his skin.

"You have to stay still." The words rushed from her.

"I will now." He closed his eyes, keeping her hand trapped. He was expecting a struggle. Instead, she snuggled down beside him. "The rain has picked up."

"Yes," she affirmed.

"I'm glad I'm not out in it."

"Would you have stayed in here tonight if you hadn't gotten hurt?"

"Yes. You were right. It would have been foolish. But it's also time … we need to talk … about …." Nathan didn't even realize his voice was fading. He was warm, tired, had Jessica beside him and he was asleep.

CRSO

Jessica awoke to the rumbling sky, and the feel of Nathan beside her. It wasn't as strange having him there as she thought it would be. In fact, she liked it. It felt good, right. She decided 'right' was the word. She shook the thought away. He was warm but not feverish, which was a relief. She lay back listening to the night sounds. In the distance Jessica thought she could hear men's voices and guessed it must be the changing of the watch and wondered if it was third or fourth watch. It had to be past the second.

Her thoughts changed to Slippers and the new foal, and she felt a stab of worry. She should've checked them out before coming back, but she had been too concerned about Nathan to think of anything else.

She lay there long enough to know she was not going back to sleep until she checked on the horses. Careful not to wake up Nathan, she slid from the bed. Once he protested, but when she laid a hand on his, he settled. Not bothering with the curtain since Nathan was asleep, she changed and climbed out.

The rain had stopped, but thick clouds hung low. The storm was not over yet.

She just prayed it would hold off until she got back in the wagon again. Pulling on her coat, she reached for the small ferry lamp, sitting just inside the gate. Jessica managed to get the candle lit and covered before the wind could blow it out.

First, she checked on the group of horses. All was well with them, so she headed between the rocks to Slippers. The mare snorted a greeting.

"Did I startle you girl?" Jessica stretched out her hand as she moved forward, rubbing her hand over the horse's side. "You had quite a day. It looks like they did get the mountain lion moved. You're probably as glad as I am for that. We both came too close to losing something precious today. But both your foal and Nathan are all right. How is the new little girl?"

The filly shied as Jessica reached out, but she was patient until it accepted her touch just as its mother did.

"Aren't you beautiful. You're going to look like your mother." Jessica ran her hand over the soft mahogany coat then touched the fine black mane, noticing the matching stubby tail. "Looks like you do have touches of your father. I hope that you keep them. Looks like you're staying pretty dry. Nathan found you a good spot. Speaking of which, I better get back to him. I'll be back in the morning." With a last check to make sure the water bucket had plenty left, she headed for the wagon.

She'd just made it past the rocks when a shadow stepped in front of her. The light crossed the man's face with barely enough time to swallow back the scream which was difficult because the sight of Emory Hayes's craggy face was not a pleasant sight in candlelight. It was only the thought of waking everyone that enabled her to muffle the outcry.

"You startled me, Mr. Hayes."

"Now what are you doing out this time of night?" There was a slur to his words, and Jessica was afraid it wasn't from sleepiness.

"I was checking on the horses."

"Heard you got another, Hawke just keeps getting more out of the marriage. But then again, I heard he got mauled by a lion. Maybe you're lookin' for a replacement tonight. He won't be any good in bed for a while. Then again, he hasn't been spending his nights inside. Maybe he wasn't any good in bed to begin with. You should have married me. I know what to do with you." The man moved in front of her.

"Mr. Hayes," Jessica found herself shifting back as he moved toward her and tried to stand her ground. "Excuse me. I need to get back, in case Nathan needs me."

Too late, she realized, it was the wrong thing to say.

His hand reached out and grabbed her arm. "What if I need you?"

Jessica started to scream again, but this time only a squeak escaped, as Hayes's big hand covered her mouth.

"I've been needin' you bad since I saw you parading around so fancy in those dresses. You should have stayed dressin' up like a boy if you didn't want attention. So I'm a think'n' you want it."

Jessica struggled to pull free, but though he was a lazy

slob, he was still powerful. With no other weapon than the ferry-lamp, she smashed it into the side of his head. The lamp broke and the flame went out, plunging them into darkness. Hayes groaned and gave her a hard shake, but didn't release her.

"You should've picked me," he growled in her face. "Light don't matter. I don't need one to do what I'm going to do to you. Then we'll just see if you be thinking you're better than me. We'll also see if Hawke still wants you. Then again, you won't tell him will you, cause we both know he would'na be want'n you."

Jessica clawed at his arm then tried for his face. Hayes stumbled back when she managed to poke his eye. One pan-sized hand hit her on the side of her head. She would have dropped if he hadn't been holding her. The ringing in her ears wiped out all other sounds. Lights flashed in front of her eyes. The next sensation she felt was falling.

Chapter Seventeen

Nathan stretched in his sleep, warm and comfortable, but the feeling that something was missing wiggled through his mind. He reached for Jessica, and when his hand came in contact with empty space, he came awake. It was only a few shades lighter then pitch-black, but enough to be able to see she wasn't there.

He waited, raising his injured arm to see how it felt. It hurt like the dickens but not as bad as he'd feared. Whatever Sanders had done to clean it, had almost taken him out, but it felt better now. He fingered above and below the bandage until satisfied with its condition. Jessica still hadn't returned.

Nathan made it into a sitting position with only one groan and reached for his pants. Once on, he decided to forgo his shirt and slicker. His coat was still covered with blood. It was hard to pull on boots one handed, but the second they were on he slid out of the wagon. He had to brace himself as the world swam in flashes of lights. When the lights condensed down to one, he focused on it.

He was sure Jessica was holding the light, but the man she was talking to had his back to him. Jessica started to move around him, but the man moved in front of her. Nathan just started their direction when the man grabbed her.

Anger gave Nathan the energy to burst into a run. He wanted to cheer Jessica when she smashed the lamp against the man's head, but the light went out. Focused on the shadows, he was only two yards away when Jessica went down from a blow of a huge hand.

The roar that burst out of Nathan probably sounded like the mountain lion's howl as he launched himself at the man. The trajectory was true. They both went down and came up swinging. Nathan hissed as a glancing blow only missed the scratches on his side by an inch.

Hayes stumbled back when Nathan's fist caught his stomach. "Should have known you'd come after her. But the way I hear it, you're all torn up. No sense getting hurt over a woman we can share. Heck, I might even be willin' to pay ya some for 'er, if she's any good."

Fury burst through Nathan, as his fist smashed into Hayes's nose. There was a crunch, but Nathan didn't pay heed. He sent his other fist to the man's stomach with enough force to lift him off the ground. Hayes dropped like a lump of lard.

Nathan dropped to the ground next to Jessica. She jerked when he touch her then launched herself into his arms. "Nathan, Nathan," she cried. Hot tears burned against his skin.

"It's all right. I have you. He's not going to hurt you."

"Nathan."

"Shh." He pressed his lips to her head.

Her hands ran over his bare chest stopping at his bandages. She pulled back. "Your stitches, you shouldn't be out of bed. It's wet out here."

"Who's out there?" A voice cut through the dark. "Nathan?"

"Is that you, Thomas?"

"Yes," a second later lantern light drew closer as the man approached. "What you doing out here? You should be in bed."

"We need help."

"Where's Emory? I woke him for watch about a half hour ago. I was just getting to sleep when I heard a ruckus."

"Hayes is over there."

"What happened to him?" The blacksmith moved to the unconscious man in concern then stopped when Nathan spoke again.

"I hit him when he attacked Jessica."

"What?" The man gaped and Jessica pressed her face against Nathan's shoulder.

"Jessica will have to tell all, but what I saw, was Jessica went out to check on the horses. On the way back, Hayes made an advance. When she tried to reject him, he grabbed her, and hit her when she tried to fight."

"Is she all right?"

"I think so. It looked like he hit her pretty hard before I could get to her."

"Looks like you landed a good one on his nose."

"He'll be lucky if that's all I do."

"Now, Nathan."

"He attacked Jessica. What would you do if it was your wife?" Nathan snarled.

"I'll tie him up. He'll face the council in the morning."

"I'll tell you this right now. If he doesn't leave, I am. I won't have Jessica put in jeopardy from him again."

"Nathan." Jessica lifted her head. In the lantern light, Nathan could make out the tears on her cheeks.

"I mean it." He cupped her chin. "I won't have him near you."

"You shouldn't be out here." She pulled herself up and reached to help him. "You're chilled. We need to get you back to bed now. What if you tore your stitches?"

Nathan realized this was Jessica's way of relieving her stress. Without a word, he let her head him back to the wagon. He accepted her help to climb in and lay back while she removed his boots. When she looked at his pants with a perplexed expression, he stopped her. "I can handle these. Why don't you light the lantern?" He didn't tell her it was so he could check on her.

She nodded and turned away. "I broke the lamp."

"It's all right. It was for a good purpose."

"You saw me hit him with it?"

"Yes, there are two more lamps packed away so we can get another one out.

"You have a lot of belongings."

"I could bring more possessions because I was only packing for me and not clothing and food for a whole family."

She nodded. Nathan slid under the quilt just as she adjusted the lantern light. "Let me see your arm."

Obediently he held it out.

"It looks fine, now your side. It looks like you've been bleeding." Anxiety tightened her voice, and she reached for the wrapping. "You pulled a couple stitches but the bleeding has stopped." She dampened a cloth and cleaned away the blood. "I'm not sure I can get a stitch in there."

Nathan looked down unconcerned. His focus had been on Jessica. There was a slight bruise around her mouth where Hayes had covered her mouth to keep her from screaming, and another on the slide of her jaw where he'd hit her, otherwise, she looked uninjured. "It will be fine. As you said, it has stopped bleeding and will hurt more to put a stitch in than it does now. How's your head?"

She put her hand up behind her ear. "It hurts a little, but my ears have stopped ringing."

"Good, why don't you lay down here? I'm still cold. You could help warm me up." Jessica moved forward then stopped. "My dress is wet."

Nathan was shocked when she reached for the buttons and removed the dress without putting up the barrier. It came to him that either she didn't want him out of her sight or didn't want to be out of his. It didn't matter to him which it was.

This time, when she slid in beside him, there was no staying close to the edge. She moved right next to him, lying along his side, her arm draped over his chest.

"Is that good?"

"Could you fix the pillow behind my head?"

Jessica leaned up and fluffed the pillow. When she settled back, her head was rested on his arm. He closed his arm around her, and she shifted naturally to his shoulder.

"Perfect." He yawned in contentment.

A shudder ran through Jessica taking with it the last of her tension and they were both asleep.

∞

It didn't take long to reach the decision that Hayes was to leave the wagon train. His defense that he'd been drinking didn't help his plea. When he tried to say Jessica had come on to him, Nathan had to be forcibly restrained.

Jacob read the verdict, but it was Richmond who chastened the man. "Emory Hayes, I suggest you search your soul and try to change your ways. You have a weakness for drink that will destroy you unless you overcome it. You are also slothful and vindictive." He pointed at him.

"Because Mrs. Hawke turned you down, you were going to take revenge in a most vile way. You are fortunate there is no law out here, and that we are too far from a fort to keep you and hand you over to them. You are also fortunate that, as men of God, we don't just string you up or shoot you. I would suggest you find God, because through him you have been saved this day."

Jacob Hammond took over. "Now you have one hour to be packed up and ready to move out."

"Move?" the man blustered. "It was declared a day of rest. The trail is a mess."

Jacob raised his hand. "You will be escorted five miles back on the trail."

"Back, you can't leave me back on my own."

"You have lost the protection of the company. If you change your ways, you may be able to join one of the ones behind us. Though we both know it is doubtful. A company is not going to accept a lone man who has been kicked out on the trail. They'll all know what kind of a man you are."

Hayes let off a string of curses then looked at Nathan. "I'll kill you, then I'll have −"

It was Hammond who cut him off. "One more word Hayes, and you will be shot." The tone in Hammond's voice must have been sufficient because Hayes shut up and Hammond continued. "Your guns and ammo have been confiscated. They will be taken back an extra mile from your wagon. You will be left with directions of how to locate them. That should add enough to your delay that we will never see you again."

Nathan watched the three men ride out escorting Hayes. Garfield rode ahead with the guns. Nathan already knew the man planned to make it hard for Hayes to find them. Nathan wished they could get away without returning them, but it would be inhumane.

He also wished he could go with them to see him gone but he needed the rest day. Last night his fury was up when he fought with Hayes, but today, he was feeling all the previous day's injuries. Though, Jessica had made a tea for him that did help his headache.

He turned and watched Jessica emerge from their wagon. After she'd been told what happened, she had elected to stay there until Hayes was gone, which suited Nathan just fine, he wanted her as far away from Hayes as possible.

When she looked toward the boulders to where Slippers and the foal were and hesitated, he turned her direction. "Would you like to join me? I thought I'd check on Slippers and move them over to the other horses so our little filly can get acquainted, then I might take a short walk. It's kind of muddy but if we're careful, we should be okay."

"It sounds wonderful."

Nathan extended his hand, and she took it. They

worked with the filly, getting her used to being handled before leading the mother and foal to the other horses.

"I don't think Jon has seen her yet. With everything going on, he's probably not heard of her birth." Nathan speculated, running his hand down the filly's neck. "How long do you think it will take him to get here when he sees her?"

"From the time he catches sight, I'm guessing twenty seconds, twenty-five at the longest. It will kill him not to run so he doesn't spook her."

Nathan laughed. "I'm sure it will be a very fast walk." They'd only been with the other horses a few minutes when an, "Oh wow," broke the air. Nathan laughed again and started counting as the six year old headed toward them.

"Twenty six," he announced. "You were off."

"But he never broke into a run. It slowed him down a little."

"Not much."

"What you talking about?" The boy tilted his head to the side as he studied the adults.

"Just foolish adult talk."

He nodded, accepting that as all the explanation he needed. "I didn't know Slippers had her baby."

"Sorry, I should have come to tell you first thing this morning. She came late last night in the storm."

"It's a filly."

"Yes."

"Have you named her yet?"

"No, I'm waiting for my helper, and of course, we need to give Nathan a vote because it's his horse, too."

"I get to help?" The boy looked to Nathan.

"Yes, you do. I'll be waiting for the names, but for now, why don't you meet her."

ભ્રજી

The next morning they were on the move. Jessica was relieved there was no sign of Hayes. Mr. Sanders took up scout so that Nathan could stay close to her. The companionship between them grew. They talked with ease on everything that came to their minds. For a time they fell silent then Nathan asked.

"Jessica, will you tell me why you ran away?"

She paused, but it was to gather her thoughts. "I need to go back a ways. I told you my father died. Well, one day my mother went to town and came back married. That was really about how it was. His name was Bradley Calloway. I still don't understand how it happened. My mother was so melancholy after my father died, I couldn't get her to do anything." She looked out over the trail.

"My grandmother and I talked her into going into town on her own. She was to shop and visit some friends. When it got late and she didn't return, we were panicked. We even had riders out searching the roads. The next day, Bradley showed up with her and announced they were married. He had the certificate to prove it. He moved into the house and tried to take over the running of The Meadows immediately."

She looked up at him. "That was when he found out that he couldn't. I inherited it all, and if anything happened to me, some distant relative in England would have gotten it. I've never heard of the person. The truth is I'm not even sure they exist, but to move on, shortly after he arrived, my grandmother died. She hadn't been ill at all and she didn't like him."

"You believe he killed your grandmother?"

"Yes, yes I do. I know it sounds unbelievable. She was old, but she was healthy, then she was gone. I have no proof though. It's all speculation. He wasn't happy when my grandmother announced that The Meadows and all the horses and money were protected. I knew she did it to protect me. She didn't trust him. The money in the money belt was my inheritance from her. She gave it to me when he moved in, late at night in my room and instructed me to sneak out and hide it."

"All that was hers?"

"Yes, and she also gave me her best jewelry, too."

"You have that with you?" It was more of a statement than a question.

"Yes, but I did hide it in your wagon the first night when you brought in the bundle it was hidden in."

"Well, thank goodness for that."

"By the way, I never found the money."

"I'll show you later," he assured her.

"To get on with it." She had to pause to calculate. "About, seven − eight weeks ago. It seems like it should be longer. My stepfather announced there was going to be a party. I thought it was unusual, but couldn't figure out what harm a party could do. I thought that it might even bring my mother out of the melancholy that had never passed. It had grown deeper, like she isn't even there most of the time, and when she does react she's not the same. The party was actually quite nice except that one of our neighbors was there that I didn't like. My father would not allow him on our property."

"I presume there was a reason?"

Jessica nodded. "When I was fifteen I was out riding, he … he attacked me. I'm not sure if I even knew what he was trying to do at the time. The only relationships I'd seen hints of were my parents, and it was loving and sweet. All I knew was I was terrified. My father had planned to meet me. He got there to save me. I thought he was going to kill Raker. I wish he would have. Raker was never allowed on our land again, and I was always watched when I went out riding. It didn't take me long to realize that. When I talked to my father about it, he explained he was afraid that Raker would come after me again."

"After your father died what happened?"

"Raker was still not allowed. Amos and the other men watched out for me."

"They had gotten used to protecting you."

"Yes, and I had quite a bit of say about the running the place, with Amos tutoring me all the way."

"Until your stepfather."

"Even after, until he managed to run Amos off. I tried to get Amos to stay. When I turned eighteen I planned on building another house and Amos could have lived there with me but Bradley kept making it difficult. There were little things that kept being done wrong or not done that were Amos's responsibility. It made it look like he was getting too old to handle his job."

"You don't believe that."

"No, I don't. I think someone was going in later and messing with them, but when someone was hurt, Amos decided he had to leave."

"How bad were you hurt?"

"How did you know it was me?"

"From what you said about Amos, he would never have left you unless he was afraid his being there put you in danger."

"You're right. He wouldn't have cared if anything happened to him. I just sprained my ankle."

"And the other time?"

"You're very good at figuring me out."

"Not you, Amos. One time wouldn't do it. One could be an accident. Twice would have been a clear warning, leave or she gets hurt. Your stepfather might not be able to kill you, but you could keep having accidents. You're lucky he didn't try to do something to incapacitate you."

"We figured it was only time. He seemed satisfied with the prestige he got with living at The Meadows, and he really didn't have to do any work. We knew the trouble would be when I turned eighteen, and had full control."

"I can't believe your father would give you full control at such a young age."

"I showed an affinity for it and by the time I was

twelve, my father already knew there was not going to be another child, no son to take over. So he started to teach me. He also set it up so I had an advisor to help. I wouldn't have been on my own until I was twenty-one. By then, I would hopefully have a husband to help me."

"I guess I can understand that. So, Amos left."

"Yes, he went to California. He wrote back that he was able to purchase two parcels of land that he put in both our names. One has a nice size home on it already and good land, perfect for horses, rich and fertile."

"Then he has what, three hundred and twenty acres?"

"Yes, and he thinks that he might be able to buy one more parcel from a person who is thinking of going back east."

"That's a lot of land, but it sounds like it might be a good place for us to settle down. What do you think Amos will think of me? I can pay my way in."

Pleasure burst inside her. "I think he'll like you a lot. You're both horsemen, and you have a code of honor he'll respect."

"That's good. I was planning on purchasing property if I found land that I wanted, instead of claiming land that wasn't as good."

"Do you mean you'll go all the way with me?"

"I'm thinking my place is with you."

"Nathan?"

"We'll talk more about that later. Right now I want you to finish telling me what made you leave."

Jessica wanted to press the other subject but guessed it wasn't the time though she really didn't want to think of the night of the party. She sighed, that was in the past. Raker couldn't hurt her now.

"I started to tell you about the party. Well, Clifford Raker was there. My stepfather had invited him. Clifford approached me when I was getting a breath of fresh air on the terrace. I got away from him and went inside. It was time for dinner so I went to my place at the table by my mother. Bradley changed me to the other side of him then Raker took the seat next to me."

"And you couldn't do anything without causing a scene."

She nodded. "Then my stepfather stood and said he had an announcement, that I would be marrying Clifford Raker the next day at noon."

"You cannot be serious."

"I tried to protest, but Clifford grabbed my arm under the table. I thought he would break it. Then he pushed my head to him, covered my mouth with his hand, said I fainted and carried me out of the room. Actually, I did faint I guess, because I woke up locked in my room. I could hear music so I knew the party was still going, but I knew I had to get out of there. There was no way I was going to marry Clifford Raker. I had the letter I'd received from Amos a month earlier. Leaving was already on my mind. So I packed my belongings."

She swallowed again as the images came to her mind. Nathan must have sensed her distress because his hand covered hers. She looked to him gaining strength.

"I was just lowering the bundles out the window when I heard the door being opened. It was Clifford. He was drunk and decided he didn't want to wait until the next day to … to claim me. I tried to tell him I wouldn't be touched before my wedding, but he just came after me." She grew silent.

"Jessica." Nathan rubbed her fingers in his.

"He was going to …" she couldn't say the word. "He threw me on the bed, and no matter what I did, I couldn't get away, then I grabbed hold of the lamp. It tipped over and hit him on the head." She caught back a sob.

"It knocked him out." Nathan figured it out.

She nodded, taking a breath to get hold of her self-control. "I tied him up and got the key. I was able to get my father's guns and sneak out of the house. It might have been foolish to take all I did and the horses, but I didn't want to leave them because I wasn't sure when, or if I'd ever return. I knew, if any of the workers caught me, they would help me get away. My only worry was my stepfather."

"So you left it all to him after all?"

"No, I made it to my father's executor. He set it so even if I'm dead, it will stay in trust for five more years. Also, I can't be declared dead for five years after my last correspondence with him."

"That was smart."

"Even if my stepfather kills me, he doesn't get The Meadows."

"You are an amazing woman, Jessica Hawke."

"I was just doing what I had to." She swallowed. "I have been so afraid." The declaration slipped out.

Nathan's arm came up around her and drew her tight to his side. "Don't be frightened. You're no longer alone, I'm with you. You're safe from Raker and your stepfather. From now on, we face everything together and I won't let anything happen to you." They fell silent with her tucked into his body as the wagon lumbered along.

Several minutes past before Nathan turned his head to brush his lips against her temple. "Jessica, we'll be making camp soon, but I want you to think of something. I'd like you to consider, if maybe, you'd be willing to be married to me for real, in every way for the rest of our lives."

When she started to answer, he stopped her. "Don't answer me now. I want you to really think about it, and I'll ask for your answer later."

Jessica thought of what he said and nothing else while they set up camp, though she already knew the answer. She would accept Nathan's new proposal because she wanted to be married to him. She loved him.

There was only one problem. Nathan hadn't said he

loved her. She was convinced he really did want her. Why couldn't someone love her; not just want her?

She looked up from preparing the food to find Nathan watching her with a breathtaking intensity. Face hot, she looked away, only to glance back a second later. This time a smile crested his lips that she would have to call wicked, but she felt no fear. Her heart sped up. There was no taking her eyes away. She was caught. She was his.

ೞೲ

Nathan worked to settle the horses and set up camp, but his attention stayed on Jessica. He was aware of everywhere she moved gathering wood. He knew how she moved. The stiffness from her injuries had left her, and she was back to her smooth fluid way, though she was still careful about lifting heavy objects. He liked the way her hips swayed when she walked, her stride would be described as far too determined to be lady like. She moved with purpose, it suited her and him.

When she went to lift the Dutch oven, he almost headed for her. It took all his will power to finish checking the hooves on the pulling team and pick up the harness to make a quick inspection before his eyes went again to his wife.

It was possible she would truly be his wife tonight. He prayed the marriage of convenience would end. After a week, it was killing him but then again he'd known from the first it wasn't what was meant to be. She was meant for him. He might not have known it at the time, but she was the reason he hadn't taken a wife before he left. He was to find her. He sent a quick prayer of thanks to the Lord for setting it up for him.

Jessica glanced his way. Even at the distance, he could see her blush and a wave of certainty swept through him. She was for him. When she looked up again, it was all he could do not to go to her, sweep her up in his arms and carry her into the woods. Then again, maybe that wasn't a bad idea, getting them away from everyone else. Nathan finished with the harness and went to prepare a few things.

Jessica placed the last items from clean up in the cooking box on the wagon when she heard hooves approach behind her. She was surprised to see Nathan on one of the horses. A pang of disappointment hit her. She'd thought they would talk about them. Then he extended his hand.

"Come for a ride with me?"

Unable to answer, she placed her hand in his, ready for him to pull her up behind him. Instead, he reached down and looped an arm around her and lifted her up in front of him with his arm staying around her waist.

They rode in silence.

Jessica thought she felt Nathan kiss the top of her head. "Where are we going?"

"Just a little farther, then we'll look for a nice spot to talk."

They fell back into silence.

"Let's try here." He led the horse into the trees. When they came to a glade, he pulled up. "This is perfect."

He swung off the saddle then raised his arms for her. Jessica placed her hands on his shoulders, and he lowered her down against him. Time stopped as they stared at each other.

"Jessica," he whispered her name an instant before his lips covered hers. The only time she had ever been kissed like this was when she had been pronounced his wife. His arms locked around her bringing her tighter to him. The kiss continued to deepen. Jessica could feel his heart pound under her hands and hers raced to match the beat. Her arms made their way up around his neck, bringing them even closer, heart to heart.

With a groan, Nathan pulled his lips from hers to run them over her cheek. He pulled back. "Jessica, I need an answer. Will you be mine?"

There was no hesitation in her. "Yes."

"Jess, I need you to be sure, absolutely certain, because once I make love to you there will be no annulment. We will be man and wife for the rest of our lives."

"Make love," she whispered. "Yes, I do want you to make love to me."

"I want to make you mine more than anything in the world."

"I want to be yours."

He kissed her hard then broke, turning to remove her bedroll from the saddle. When he reached for her hand, she was nervous, but certain of her actions as she went with him.

掘

Jessica lay nestled in Nathan's arms, staring at the stars visible through the trees. Again she felt Nathan press his lips to her temple. She turned to look at him. "I'm yours now."

He cupped her face in his hands. In the moonlight she could see his smile. "Yes."

"Is it always like this between a man and a woman?"

"Only when it's right, that was special, and it will get better. All I'll ever give you is pleasure when I come to you."

"I wasn't sure what to expect, but I thought that was pleasurable."

She felt Nathan laugh. His lips touched her temple again. "So did I."

"I love you."

"I love you too." He pulled her over him and kissed her. "I should get you back to the wagon."

"Can't we stay here?"

"You don't want to get back to a nice feather bed?"

"I don't want to leave your arms."

"Believe me, I don't plan to let you out of my reach. Tomorrow's the Sabbath and I plan on spending the whole day just holding you."

"I like the sound of that."

"Good, because I'm afraid I may have trouble keeping my hands off my wife." His hands moved over her back proving his words. He ran one hand through her hair bringing her head down so he could catch her lips.

"I could kiss you forever, but we really must get back."

This time Nathan lifted her up into the saddle then swung up behind her. Back at camp she waited for him to unsaddle the horse. The instant he finished he took her hand, and they went to the wagon together. Jessica snuggled back into Nathan's arms and sighed with contentment.

"Go to sleep, Mrs. Hawke," Nathan whispered in the darkness.

"Goodnight, Mr. Hawke."

"It's been a very good night." He tightened his hold and shifted to give her one last kiss.

୦ଓ୫୦

"You seem to have finally settled into married life." Sara gave her a knowing smile as they prepared for the potluck the next day.

Jessica couldn't keep back the blush. "Is it obvious?"

"That you look like a woman who's been well and thoroughly made love too. Yes, and it doesn't hurt that Nathan is strutting around like a very satisfied stallion. He also keeps a very close eye on you. I swear this is the first time he's been more than two feet from your side, and I had to get Jacob to waylay him for that." Sara lowered her voice. "I wanted to check on how you were doing. The first time can be a bit traumatic for a young woman."

Jessica blushed. "I'm fine. Nathan's been very caring." Her blush deepened. "He even explained some of the things to me so I wouldn't be so nervous."

"Smart man. Good man."

"Yes, so I'm doing fine."

"Well, if you have any questions let me know. I could use the practice. It won't be long until I'll have to explain it to Molly. Heavens, time does go by. Oh, it looks like time to end our talk, here's Nathan to claim you."

A second later Nathan's hand settled on her back.

Chapter Eighteen

"Do you think we can catch a fish before Nathan gets here?" Jon looked to Jessica, his blue eyes beaming with excitement.

"I'd say so, though he wants a chance to catch some so we better not catch them all." The last four days the trail hadn't followed a river. Tonight, they were back on the river. Jessica decided to take a chance to have fish for dinner. Of course, when Jon heard she was going fishing, he was ready to go. Nathan unfortunately had to help Mr. Ford with an axle problem.

"Nathan didn't think it looked too bad. He thought it would only take him and Mr. Sanders an hour to have it fixed." Jon had a way of knowing everything.

"Nathan told me the same thing." She relaxed back against the bank, happy and content, letting Jon ramble on.

"Nathan's coming already."

Jessica heard footsteps, but knew they were too loud to be Nathan's. "It's not Nathan. Someone else probably decided to have fish for supper."

"Papa and Joseph went up stream. He took Kimball with him to give Mama a break."

Jessica knew she was hearing just how it had been said.

"Ain't that good to know. It means we're less likely to be disturbed. Would ya look at that? Hayes here was right. The boy was a woman, and I'm bettin' he was tellin' the truth when he said, her name was really Jessica Wellington."

"Her name is Jessica Hawke." Jon jumped to his feet in front of her. Even at his age, he sensed danger and was ready to champion her.

"Jon get back," Jessica pulled him back, placing both hands on his shoulders. She recognized the men that tried to buy then steal the horses.

"Told you it was her," Emory Hayes moved down the river bank into view.

They were effectively trapped between the men and the river.

"If you're interested in horses, you'd have to talk to my husband."

"Letting him make the decisions after all?" Hayes sneered.

"We're no longer interested in the horses. Found something that pays better." The thinner man, named Stubbs, said as he moved forward. "It seems someone is offering a lot of money for you."

Sickness welled inside her. Her stepfather had put out a bounty for her. "You're too late, he won't pay now. It's no good. I'm of age and married."

"The bounty didn't mention any conditions like that."

"I promise it's null now." She tried to convince them as the semi-circle closed in.

"You really expect us to believe you?"

"Look, I'll pay you what is offered. How much is it."

"You're worth one hundred dollars."

"Then I'll give you one hundred and twenty."

The men laughed. "You don't have that kind of money."

"I can get ..." She was cut off.

"Get the woman."

"What do we do with the boy?"

"Throw him in the river and drown him. Maybe they'll think she did it then ran off."

"No," Jessica screamed. "Run, Jon." She threw herself

at the men, clawing like a wild cat, hitting and screaming. Out of the corner of her eye, she saw one of the men grab for Jon and propelled herself at him, tackling the man as Jon ran past.

Jessica and Stubbs both slipped off the bank. The man landed in knee deep water, Jessica sprawled in the muddy edge. Rough hands grabbed the back of her dress hauling her up, but she didn't notice the rough treatment as she watched Jon speed away. Hayes tried to go after him, but it was quickly obvious he wouldn't catch the boy.

"The whelp got away," he huffed back.

"It's okay. We got what we need. Let's get out of here."

"We'd better make it fast. The boy'll go right to Hawke and he'll be on us. He won't give up until he gets her back or is dead."

"Then we'll help him get dead."

"No," Jessica burst with fury, trying to free herself. She didn't see the blow coming so there was no way to stop it before the world was lost in darkness.

ः

"Nathan! Nathan! Nathan!"

Nathan was crouched next to the wagon wheel when he heard the voice yelling his name. As soon as he saw Jon running toward him and no sign of Jessica, he knew there was trouble. He was at a full run when he caught Jon up in his arms, outside the camp.

"Jon, what is it? What happened to Jessica?" he yelled, still searching for signs of her over the boy's head.

"They took her." The boy gulped air.

"They?" Nathan's mind went to Indians, but there hadn't been problems with them.

"Who took her?"

"Mr. Hayes and those two men that wanted the horses."

"Hayes?"

Jon nodded. "They said something about him being right, that Jessica was the right woman. They said they were going to drown me. Jess yelled at me to run and jumped on them. I wanted to help but I ran because that was what Jess wanted me to do. I knew she wanted me to get you."

"Good boy." Nathan was already running with Jon in his arms. "You have to show me where you were."

"We were down around the bend. There's a nice deep hole. They came out of the willows."

He stopped and put the boy down. "Jon, I want you to go back to your mother and tell her what happened." He could see several of the other men who had heard the yelling, following him.

With the boy headed back to camp, Nathan rounded the bend, homing in on the fishin' hole. There was no sign of Jessica or the men, but plenty of footprints to show he was in the right place. Nathan turned to one of the men coming up behind him. "See how far you can follow the tracks. I'm going back for Titan."

It took less than three minutes for him to get to his horse and back to see the man waving to him. "Nathan, it looks like they had horses tied up in those trees. They came this way. It's faint, but the ground's soft enough you can make out the trail."

Nathan could see what the man was talking about.

"Give us a minute, and we'll saddle up and go with you."

"Just catch up with me." He urged Titan forward as fast as he dared. At one point he lost the trail until he found signs where they tried to wipe the tracks out. After another fifty feet, it became clear again. Nathan took time to mark it for the men who followed after him, then was on his way again.

He gave a prayer of thanks that there were not a lot of shoed horses in the area or he would never have been able to distinguish the track. Then he added a prayer that Jessica would be safe until he reached her.

ೞೕ

Jessica came awake to the heavy smell of a sweating horse and a nauseating motion from being draped over the back of the animal. Each of the horse's steps jarred the air from her lungs. A crushing fear clamped down when she remembered what was happening. Bradley Calloway had put out a bounty on her, and she was going to be taken to him. Be taken away from Nathan.

She wondered what Calloway would do when he found out she was married, and couldn't force her into marriage or have control of her. She wondered if he would let her go then figured the answer was no. After sending men this far after her, he was not a man to give up and admit defeat. She had underestimated him and now she feared for Nathan. He was in danger because of her.

Her stomach churned at the thought of Nathan, combined with it already being unsettled by the motion and her head hanging down, she barely got her head up before the first wave of sickness flowed forth.

"She's sick." One of the men yelled and the horses stopped. They waited for the first bout to end before untying her.

Jessica slumped to the ground as soon as her feet touched it and fought to keep from being ill again.

"We need to get out of here," Hayes grumbled. "We're not far enough away. Hawke will be after us by now."

"I covered our trail, and it's not likely he's an experienced enough tracker to follow us. Besides, let him come, we'll take care of him."

"Hawke isn't stupid. He'll know you're expecting him, but he'll come after the woman anyway. Nothing will stop him."

"Just cause he bested you," Jacks sneered, "that don't take much."

"I had my reasons throwing in with you."

"What is it you want?" Stubbs asked.

"To get even with Hawke and to get what's comin' to me from her." Hayes jerked his arm toward Jessica. "But first we need to put some more distance between us."

"I can't," Jessica gasped out. Her stomach had settled, and though she ached, she was feeling better.

"You'll do what you're told." Hayes stepped forward, grabbing her hair to pull her up.

Jessica cried out, but it was Stubbs that came to her aid. "Don't hurt her. She's to be taken care of or we won't get paid."

"I ain't hurting her, just getting her back on the horse."

"Please no, I'll be sick again."

"Let her sit up," Jacks suggested.

"I'm putting her with you," Stubbs said to him.

The man shrugged and turned to Jessica. "You better not be pukin' on me or you'll be tied on the back again."

Jessica longed to run, but her legs were still too shaky to hold her and a few minutes later, she was boosted onto the horse with Jacks.

"I should've taken her," Hayes grumbled in his forever complaining tone.

"Shut up," Stubbs snapped, causing the horse and Jessica to jump. Contention between the men was obvious. But what frightened her most was she was being taken farther from Nathan. Twice she was able to hold them up pretending to be sick.

Jessica figured they planned to travel until dark and wasn't prepared when they swung deep into a forest area. Then she saw Hayes's wagon.

This time she was pulled from the horse only to be forced down by a tree and have her hands tied behind her back. When she complained about the bark digging into her, she got no response.

"We should get movin'," Hayes spoke up.

"You want to leave your wagon?"

"I don't care about it. I can always come back for it."

"It'd be gone," Stubbs said.

"So what, he's already drunk all his supplies. What's he need it for?" Jacks jeered.

"We need it to take her back," Stubbs countered. "There'll be a lot less questions with the wagon."

"Nobody's gonna believe we're going back cause she's sick, if they see her tied up," Hayes argued.

"Then we don't let them see her."

"You don't know busybodies on wagons. They have to get their noses in everything. I say we get movin' and just stay off the trail with her."

"Well, you don't get a say. Now fix us somethin' to eat."

Hayes started grumbling under his breath, but he went to work on putting together food. "Ought to make her do it, she's good at cookin'."

Hayes looked over at her. Jessica felt her skin crawl under his gaze and looked away. She heard his disgusting chuckle, but refused to look back.

Stubbs brought food to her. He untied her hands and shoved it at her before he started talking. "So what makes you so valuable that some'un would pay to get you back?"

She looked up and glared. "My stepfather wants my inheritance. He has to have me to get it. He can't even pay you without me."

"That right?"

"Yes, I'm telling you the truth. If you want money for me; get a message to my husband. He'll pay you the money." She accentuated the words, "To get me back."

"If your husband can get the money, why would he need you?"

"I don't think you'd understand," she bit out.

The man scowled a moment then looked her over. "Oh, I understand why a man would want you, but you can buy a whole lot of that for what we'll be getting for you. Yes'un, we can settle back and do a lot of relax'un for what we're gettin' for you."

"You won't get anything out of him."

When Jessica showed no signs of eating, he re-tied her hands and left. Jessica leaned her head back against the tree and fought to hold in the tears. She wouldn't let them see her cry.

She wanted Nathan, but was afraid of what would happen to him if he showed up. There was no doubt the men would kill him. And if she didn't get away, Nathan would come for her.

He would give up going to California to search until he found her.

Jessica opened her eyes and studied her surroundings.

From the ride in, she knew they weren't far from the trail. There was plenty of growth, but she thought she knew about where they were. She remembered the big forested area they had skirted. It ran up into some low rolling hills. If she could get away, there would be plenty of places to hide in the thick growth – if she could get away.

With a glance to check on the men, she started working on rubbing the rope against the tree. It stung her skin where the rope and the tree bit into her flesh. She heard someone clanging by the wagon and looked over to check where the men were.

They had finished eating. Jacks was nowhere in sight. Stubbs sat back with his eyes closed. Hayes was shoving things into the wagon. He turned to catch her watching and a malicious smile crossed his face. He threw out his chest then rubbed his hands over his pot belly. Jessica turned away from the disgusting man.

At the sound of footsteps approaching, she lifted her head. Seeing only Hayes, she looked away again.

"Still think you're better than me? Well, it's time to show you different."

Jessica ignored his words until he knelt and put his hand down on her knee. "Don't touch me." She pulled back and glared at him.

"Oh, I'm going to do more than touch you." He clamped down with his fingers.

"No!" Jessica kicked out, but he caught her ankle.

"You can fight all you like. I'll enjoy it all the more when I have you."

"No." She tugged and kicked out with her other foot.

"Hayes, leave'er alone."

"I've been want'n her." He leaned forward pinning her leg under his, and then let out an "oof" when she caught him in the stomach with her knee.

Jessica tasted blood when he slapped her and screamed when his filthy hand locked on her other leg.

"I said, let her be," Stubbs ordered, standing up.

"If you don't want to hear her, get me a rag to shut her up with."

"The word was she was not to be hurt or touched. Or the man won't pay."

"He won't know. She's been giv'n it to Hawke."

Jessica screamed again when he started to push her dress up to her knees. A shot rang out, cutting off her scream, which started right up again when Emory Hayes fell forward over her legs, a red bloodstain spreading over the back of his shirt.

"I should have done that as soon as he pointed you out. The worthless –"

Another shot rang out cutting off what the man was saying. Stubbs dropped to the ground, clutching his shoulder.

03❧80

Nathan found where someone had been sick and knew it was Jessica. He just wondered what they did to her to make her ill since she hadn't been earlier. Jon hadn't said they knocked her out, but knowing her, she would fight

ALYSIA S. KNIGHT

them all the way if she was conscious.

He picked up the pace. Since the one effort to hide their tracks, they seemed to give up on the need. Either they were over-confident fools, complete idiots, or they were waiting for him. Nathan was guessing it was the latter but figured it could be a combination of all three.

Two more places showed signs of stopping before he followed the tracks into the trees. He left Titan at the edge to go forward on foot, scouting the area so he didn't walk into a trap. It wasn't long before he found the markings from a wagon that had to belong to Hayes, and he continued on in a circular pattern.

The smell of smoke from a camp fire told him he was getting close. He slowed, moving as silently a possible, hoping for the advantage of surprise. The scream that split the air almost stopped his heart. He hunched low and ran forward, his need to get to Jessica out weighing caution. When Jessica screamed again, it was very near, he quickened his pace.

A shot rang out stopping him cold. *Jessica*, he raced forward. Jessica came into view as she screamed again. Nathan registered the scene in an instant. Locking in on the man with a gun pointed at her, Nathan raised his own pistol and shot. The man went down clutching his shoulder. Nathan jerked as Jessica screamed again but stayed focused on the man with a gun.

"Drop your gun." He moved closer. "Kneel down with your hands up."

"My shoulder."

"Kneel down. Feel lucky I didn't kill you like you did Hayes."

With the man on the ground, Nathan came forward and picked up his gun.

"Where's your partner?"

"Gone out watching for you."

Nathan studied the area before moving to his wife.

"Jessica?"

Tears filled her eyes as she stared at the dead man sprawled across her legs. "Jessica love." He knelt beside her.

"Can you get him off me? I can't move him." Her voice was oddly detached. Nathan laid both guns down, lifted Hayes, and dragged his body behind the trees, so he was out of her sight. It was when he came back that he realized her arms were tied around the tree, that she wasn't just keeping them back so she didn't have to touch Hayes.

"Oh, love, I'm sorry." He knelt over her, pulled his knife, and reach behind to cut her free.

"Nathan." Her face pressed into his chest. The instant he released her arms, they locked around him.

"I was afraid you'd come, and they'd kill you."

"I'm fine, but we have to get out of here before the other man gets back." He rubbed his hands up and down her back, all the while keeping an eye on the man he'd shot. Nathan knew he needed to check the man. But for a minute, Jessica needed him more and he needed to hold her. Nathan shifted to kiss her but he caught a movement through the trees. The reach for his gun was stopped by a sharp command.

"Don't move. Throw your gun over here." Jacks waited while he complied. "So Hayes was right, you did come after her. I thought the man was just whining. But you did stay close and made it real difficult to get to her. You all right?" he called to his partner.

"He shot me, Jacks. Shoot him."

"Looks like he shot Hayes, too. Good riddance."

"Nathan didn't shoot him, he did." Jessica indicated to Stubbs.

"What are you complaining about? Did you a favor." Stubbs snapped. "He wanted you and wouldn't listen when I told him to leave you alone."

"It was no matter. We was gonna get rid of him

anyway. Now why don't you," Jacks indicated to Nathan, "move away from the little lady. Isn't that a hoot. I thought she was a boy before, though it sure did have us wondering with those horses. Now move, we don't want her getting' hurt."

"No," Jessica threw herself between them. Nathan took the opportunity to pick up Stubbs' gun that had lain hidden on the other side of him. Jacks saw it too late. Nathan fired just as Jacks started to aim. Jacks' shot went wild as Nathan's found it mark. He pulled Jessica into his arms again, shifting so she didn't have to see the dead man.

"Are there any others?"

She shook her head. "No."

He kissed her forehead then held her back. "I want you to stay here. I have to check on Stubbs here or whatever his name is." He stood then froze, his hand going back to the gun he had put in the holster, as two men from the wagon train stepped into view. Nathan relaxed. "I'm glad to see you."

"Looks like you got your wife back." Thomas, a thin man about Nathan's age, commented as Nathan came back over to slide his arms around Jessica. "What's happened here? You got them all. I didn't know you were that good with a gun."

"I'm not. The man over there shot Hayes before I got here. I shot him. I thought he was about to shoot Jessica next. While I was untying her, the other one showed up. He didn't know I had his partner's gun and was able to shoot him before he shot me."

"Well, I guess we better bury Hayes and the other man. What do we do with him?" Mr. Ford motioned to the man whose shoulder he was bandaging.

Nathan took a minute to think. "We should be coming up on a fort in another week and a half. I guess we can take him there and let them figure out what to do with him."

"He'll probably just hang. You should have just killed

him and saved them the trouble," Thomas pointed out.

"I'd rather leave it to the law."

"I'll agree with that," Mr. Ford put in.

"What about Hayes's wagon? It'd be a waste to leave it here," Jessica spoke up finally, though her voice still trembled.

It was Ford that came up with the answer. "I suggest we take it with us and let the council decide."

"I agree." Nathan nodded. "But I'd like to get Jessica away from here."

"Can't blame you for that," Mr. Ford said. "We'll take care of the burying and getting the wagon and him back. There's a full moon tonight, so even if we don't make it before dark, we'll be right as rain."

"You're sure?"

"You need to get your lady out of here," Thomas voiced.

"Thank you. Come on." He reached to help Jessica up then wrapped his arm around her. She leaned on him as they walked. Her quietness worried him as did the fact that she was none too steady on her feet. "It's not far now."

"I'm fine, I just feel a little weak."

"I know you were sick."

"When I woke up I found they had tied me over the back of a horse."

"So they did knock you out. I figured you wouldn't go without a fight."

"I didn't want to leave you." When tears came to her eyes, Nathan stopped and pulled her into his arms. She clung to him. "They were taking me to my stepfather. He has a bounty out on me."

He tilted her chin so their eyes met. "No man will ever take you from me again. I love you. I plan to have a long life together."

"Oh, Nathan, I love you too. I can't believe this happened to me. When my father died and everything changed, I kind of gave up on the thought that I'd ever find anyone to love. The night I ran away, I totally gave up on my chances."

"I believe sometimes the Lord has his plans for us, and we just have to have faith and let them happen. I know I am thankful for you." He kissed her until she was breathless and weak against him for a totally different reason than before.

When they reached Titan, he lifted her into the saddle then swung up behind her. She nestled back against his chest and fell asleep. Nathan kept Titan's pace slow, appreciating the animal's smooth gait more than ever.

It was all the yelling that he was coming with her that woke Jessica. The bewildered look that came over her as she got her bearings made him smile, then the look she gave him took his breath away, there was such love and trust in her eyes. He was filled with an overwhelming need to make love to her, to reassure himself that she was fine. He wanted to carry her right to the wagon, but they were surrounded as he lifted her down.

"Jess, Jess." Jon threw his arms around her legs, hugging her. He looked up when she touched his head. "I ran just like you told me, all the way to Nathan."

She crouched down to hug the small boy she'd come to love. "You did just right. Thank you for helping Nathan rescue me."

"Are you all right?"

"Yes, just tired."

"I was real scared."

"I was scared myself. I'm happy to be back."

"Did you get them?" Jon asked Nathan with the exuberance that only a child could muster in that situation.

"Yes, one of them killed Mr. Hayes."

"Where are the other men?" Mr. Ford's wife asked anxiously.

"They were going to bury Hayes and the other man

that I shot, and then they'll bring the other man and Hayes's wagon."

"So, it was the horse thieves?" Jacob Hammond asked.

"Yes, the two men that Jessica stopped that night."

"Now that's enough for now," Sara spoke up. "Jessica has had a harrowing experience. Nathan, why don't you take her to your wagon to rest? She'll want you there with her. There'll be plenty of time to talk when the other men get here. Everyone, just give them some time. Nathan, you come get something to eat when you're ready."

"Thank you, Sara." He lifted Jessica into his arms and carried her through the crowd as it parted.

"I can walk."

"I know, but I need to hold you."

"Nathan?"

"I really need to hold you." His need must have shown on his face because when he looked down, she blushed. "Is that all right?" His voice grew husky and he swallowed hard.

Her blush deepened. "Yes."

"If you're uneasy and want some time, I can wait."

Her fingers came to his lips to stop the words. "No, there's no need to wait."

He lifted her inside the wagon and followed her in.

Jessica was asleep when Hayes's wagon rolled in. Nathan dressed to come out, though he hated leaving Jessica.

It was dark, but the crowd gathered again.

"Nathan," the men greeted.

"You had trouble?" He knew the answer was going to be yes.

"We lost Stubbs. I was hitching up the wagon …" Mr. Ford took over the explanation, "while Thomas went to get our horses. I thought Stubbs was unconscious, but when my back was turned, he snuck away. I don't know how he ever made it onto a horse without me hearing."

Nathan nodded and glanced toward the wagon where Jessica slept. "Don't worry about it. He's in no condition to try to come after her again. He'll be lucky if he survives without care." Nathan found the words reassuring to himself but made a mental oath to keep a close eye on Jessica.

Chapter Nineteen

Jessica couldn't believe she could have slept in so late. If she didn't hurry, they wouldn't get breakfast before Sunday service. The thought of food made her stomach tighten and roll, but Nathan must be starving.

This was the second time in just three days he had let her sleep in. Just the morning before last, Nathan had risen, eaten, loaded up the horses, and had them already for the trail before she'd awaken.

He had waved her concerns about oversleeping away. Saying she obviously needed the sleep. She had to admit she did. She didn't know why she was so tired, but she didn't want everyone to think she was slacking. It was enough that Nathan was so overprotective of her he hardly let her out of his sight. Now she was sleeping in half the day.

Jessica did up the laces on her boots and swung her legs over the side of the wagon in a sudden movement that sent the blood rushing to her head. Lights flashed in front of her eyes and everything blurred. *I'm going to faint.* The thought hit her as she went limp and dropped to the ground missing the desperate grab she made for the tailgate by inches.

ᚗᚙ

"Nathan, Nathan."

Nathan was surprised to see Joseph Hammond running toward him calling his name instead of his younger brother. A spear of panic that something had happened to Jessica shot through him, but he managed to push it away. Jessica was safely asleep in their wagon. He had checked on her right before coming down to wash up and shave.

Nathan wiped his face on the toweling and waved to the boy.

"Nathan," Joseph yelled, "something's wrong with Miss Jessica."

Nathan felt his heart lurch then begin to pound as he broke into a run, leaving his belongings lying on the bank. A half a dozen people were gathered around the back of his wagon, but to his relief, Jessica was sitting in the middle of them on a box that had been placed on the ground.

"Jess." Nathan skidded to a stop and she turned to him.

"I'm fine," she said, but her face was flushed.

"What is it?" He came forward, and knelt beside her. Picking up one hand to hold in his while, he brushed her cheek with his other.

"It's just foolishness. I hopped out of the wagon too fast. The blood rushed to my head, and I got a little dizzy."

"You fainted," Sara said, over her shoulder.

"I ... I just felt dizzy."

"And your stomach, how's it feeling?" the woman pried.

"Fine, maybe a little off but I'm hungry. I didn't feel like eating much last night. Someone was cooking fish, and I don't know what they did but the smell bothered me."

Nathan took his eyes off Jessica long enough to catch Sara's nod and she smiled at him. "Get that worried look off your face, she's fine. Why don't you help her back into the wagon, and I'll dish up some food for her to eat."

"I just got up," Jessica objected.

Sara ignored her. "Why don't you lie down until you've had something to eat? Then you can get back up." Sara shoed her family away while Nathan helped Jessica rise.

"Nathan, I don't need to lie down. I have things I need to do."

"Just for a minute." He employed what he found worked really well with her. "For me, so I don't worry." He leaned forward and kissed her. She sighed, gave in and took his hand so he could help her in.

Once Jessica was settled, he headed for the older woman. "Sara, what's wrong with her?"

"I'd say nothing, she's young and healthy. She should be just fine."

"What do you mean should be? Why is she so tired? She slept for over a mile on the trail the other day. She hasn't done that since she was injured. Is it something to do with that?" He voiced what he'd feared for days.

This time the woman laughed. "Not at all," then she sighed. "I really should wait until you two figure it out yourselves, but I'm afraid you'll worry yourself sick first, so let me say this. You're as good as that stallion of yours."

"Titan, what …?" The thought hit him, stopping him cold. *Could she?* Joy rushed through his every pore.

"You never did get paid for that stud fee did you? This should more than make up for it. Though I can say from experience there are times when Jessica's not going to think it was a fair trade. When she figures you got the fun without any of the discomfort."

"Jessica's pregnant."

"As much experience as you have with horses, you should have figured that was going to happen sooner or later. It just looks like it was sooner."

Nathan felt himself redden. "My first wife, we'd been married nearly a year and a half, and it never happened."

"I don't know what to say about that, but I'm willing to bet Jessica is expecting. When was her last monthly time?"

Heat burned in his face. "She hasn't had one since we …"

"She had one when she was injured so she really should be due for one soon. You'll have to ask her to be certain."

Again he flushed, and Sara laughed a full deep rolling laugh. "You better go talk to your wife. I'm afraid it may take Jessica a while to figure it out. She's kind of innocent that way."

"She told me her mother had trouble getting pregnant, and she hadn't explained to Jessica about being with a man."

"I know, she mentioned that to me."

"Thank you, Sara."

The woman waved him off. "You remind me of my younger brother. I had about the same conversation with him two years back. It's hard leaving family behind, so I'm making a new one."

Nathan understood what she was saying. They were her family now. "Thank you." He stepped forward to place a kiss on her cheek.

"Oh, you." This time Sara blushed. "Go on and take this to your wife to eat." She handed him a bowl and hurried off. Nathan smiled after her then his smile broadened. Jessica was with child. He hurried over to the wagon.

Nathan was surprised she was actually laying down when he entered. He couldn't take his eyes away from her. It was hard to believe she could be carrying his child.

Jessica opened her eyes and met his look, a smile bowed her lips. "Nathan," his name was breathless. He like the sound of it. "Is something wrong?"

"No, I was just thinking about how beautiful you are."

Her smile brightened. "Thank you."

"How are you feeling now?"

"I'm fine. I was fine before. I don't know what happened. I just can't understand why I'm so tired lately."

"But you're feeling good?"

"Yes." She sat up. "Please don't worry."

"I'm not. I just want you to be careful and get lots of

rest."

"I'm not sick, and I'm all healed up. The last of my bruises have been gone for over a week."

"I'm aware of that but, Jessica, I want to ask you something." He couldn't believe he was uncomfortable asking her this. So he blurted it out. "When was your last monthly time?"

"Monthly time?" she repeated, then blushed as he had with Sara. "You think it's my time. No, I don't get sick for that. I know it bothers a lot of women, but mine's not bad, it just comes kind of close, twenty-one days ..." her voice faded away, her eyes went wide, and a hand went to her stomach. "I haven't had it since we ... you think ... I'm ...?" A smiled blossomed across her face. "I'm going to have your baby."

Nathan knew he too was smiling. "I think it's a strong possibility. What do you think?"

"I don't know. I'm only maybe a couple days late. Though I don't ever remember being late before. Oh my, you really think?"

"That it's possible, yes. I guess we wait for a couple days more to be certain. Will you please take care until we figure it out for sure?"

"Yes. Nathan, it's all right if I'm with child, isn't it? I mean, I know it's soon. We're just married, and it'll take us two months more to reach California and—"

He cut her off by placing his mouth over hers in a hard, passionate kiss. "It's not only fine, I think it's wonderful. I like the thought of my baby ..." he paused, sliding his hand over hers on her stomach, "growing here. In fact, now I think of it. If you aren't carrying my baby yet, I just might have to try my best to make it so."

"I thought what you've been doing was pretty perfect as is." There was an unmistakable gleam in her eye.

"Cheeky, but I thank you. Believe me it has been my pleasure."

Cƺ୨ଠ

A couple days later when her monthly time still had not come, Jessica worked up enough courage to talk to Sara about the possibility of being pregnant.

"Time is really the only way to know for certain," Sara explained. "Not every woman gets sick. You might be one of the fortunate ones that don't have much of that."

"My mother had an awful time. They put her to bed almost as soon as they knew she was carrying a child, and she would still lose it. I'm the only one she carried to the end. After a while, the doctor cautioned my parents to avoid letting her get pregnant."

"Do you take after her?"

"No, not really, I favor more my father and grandmother Wellington."

"Did she have trouble?"

"No, she used to say she was working in the garden when she went into labor once and was helping build a fence another time."

"Maybe you'll be like her. I actually do quite well, though I do spend quite a few mornings sick. The trick is to eat a little, like dry bread, before you rise, that helps."

Jessica remained fine for three more days until she was preparing some fish for dinner that she, Nathan, and Jon caught when they stopped that evening. Nathan was shifting packs under the wagon. One minute she was fine, the next she was barely able to get away from the camp before she was ill. The next thing she knew, Nathan was there beside her.

"I'd say your short hair is a blessing right now," he said, once he'd wiped her face with his handkerchief and settled her back into his arms.

Her head lay on his chest, but she tipped it so she could look up to him. "The fish, I couldn't take the smell, it just hit me."

He leaned his forehead down to hers. "My poor love. I

guess if I want fish for the next couple months, I'll have to cook it myself, somewhere away from you."

"But I like fish."

"I'll cook it for you, and we'll see how that goes."

"Oh, the fish will burn." She drew away.

"I pulled the pan off the fire but I'll check it. Why don't you settle down in the shade there and I'll finish up supper."

Chapter Twenty

Jessica looked around at the large cluster of people. Their company had arrived at the fort earlier that day. They were going to take two days of down time while Mr. Garfield used the smith's forge to make some repairs to wagon pieces that had broken and had been jury rigged to reach this point. She and Nathan had covered the charge for the use of the forge allowing their company to stay.

There was another wagon train there for the same reason and would be leaving in the morning, but for the evening, they were joining with the other camp and with people from the fort for dinner and dancing.

Jessica glanced over to where Nathan stood talking to the fort's commander and several other men. He had told her when it was time to go get the Dutch oven to let him know, and he would go with her to carry it. Now that they decided she was indeed pregnant, he had relaxed, but was still overprotective about what she did.

Nathan looked totally involved in the discussion, and Jessica decided there was no need to disturb him to carry over the apple bread pudding, that was her contribution to the meal. It was easy to slip out of the crowd, and she sighed in relief for the moment of peace. She skirted the first group of wagons to where her and Nathan's wagon was parked. She felt a rush of pleasure. They were a couple now. They worked together well. Life was good, great as far as she was concerned. A feeling of contentment rushed through her.

Around the back of the wagon, she moved directly to

the fire pit and used a stick to brush back the coals. That was when she realized Sara's oven already sat out of the pit they decided to share to conserve wood use.

"Sara." She looked around for her friend. A second later Sara appeared. She seemed stiff and her eyes filled with tears. "Sara?" Jessica took a step in her direction.

Sara raised a hand, "Jessica." Her body shook. "I'm sorry." Sara stumbled forward, shoved away from the man that stepped into the clearing.

"Clifford." Jessica's eyes went to the boy he held in front of him then to the face of the man whom she feared more than any other.

"Jess." Jon's voice was muffled from the huge hand that covered half his face.

"How accommodating of you. I thought I would have to draw you out to get you alone. I found a reluctant volunteer but once I explained it was in her son's best interest."

"Let them go."

"I will once I have you on your way back home."

Jessica glanced around nervously trying to hold in her dread. "Where's Bradley?" she added, stalling for the time to think.

"Calloway? I'm sure he's back at your estate hiding out, trying to keep your mother as happy and content as possible now that you've escaped his control. The swine has been cowering since your lawyer visited and explained you and your money were out of reach, and there was no way to get you back before you turned eighteen. And if he wanted to continue to live comfortably at Wellington Meadows, he would cease all action against you or he'd be left without a penny."

A wave of relief hit her so profound that she almost sank to her knees until her mind came up against a block. "If it wasn't Bradley Calloway that offered the bounty on me, than who?" Her eyes locked back onto Raker. "You!

Why? You can't make me marry you."

"Of course, you will marry me. You should've been married to me years ago. You were meant to be mine. If your father hadn't stood in my way, I would have had you. But even after I got rid of him, I couldn't get near you."

"Got rid … you killed my father."

"He was in my way. He caught me trying to get to you. His horse reared up as I shot. The bullet should have killed him, but it worked out just as well. When he fell, the rock was right there and it left no question."

"You killed him." Jessica rushed at him only to freeze when he pulled Jon out in front of him, locking his arm around Jon's neck, making him gag.

"No," Sara screamed.

"None of that." Raker scowled, and Sara clamped her mouth shut but Jessica took up the plea.

"No, please don't hurt him."

"Then you will do as I say."

Defeated, Jessica nodded.

"Very good, I knew you could be reasonable. I should have thought of it sooner. Now get that rope there and tie up the woman and gag her with your bonnet. I don't want her yelling for help."

With weighted feet, Jessica moved forward. "I'm so sorry. I didn't know," she pleaded for forgiveness from her friend.

"Tie her to the end of the wagon and make it tight or the boy will pay."

The cringe was automatic as he moved up behind her. Jessica debated turning and trying to grab Jon free but knew she couldn't risk it. Clifford would think nothing of hurting Jon. He had killed her father just to get to her. She fought back a sob as she tied Sara's hands.

"Good, now gag her." The instant Jessica pulled the bonnet from her head Raker's hand locked in her hair yanking it back. "What have you done to your hair?" The words were demanding as he jerked with every syllable.

"I cut it to hide from you." She let out her own anger.

He leaned forward placing his mouth by her ear. "He said you disguised yourself as a boy. That was why it took so long to find you."

She fought back another sob feeling his breath touch her neck. "Who told you?" She got the words out by focusing on tying the bonnet around Sara's mouth, leaving it as loose as she dared.

"The man your guard shot. By the way, I finished him off for you. He was going to die anyway. I just helped him along."

Another sinking feeling rushed through her, bringing tears for a man who was a horse thief, kidnapper, and killer, but who also had saved her even if it was for a selfish motive.

"Good, now tie up the boy's hands."

Jessica swiped away the tears and knelt in front of Jon, but before she could start, Jon bit down on Clifford's hand. Clifford yelled and cursed. Jessica pulled Jon free then froze when the hammer of the pistol was pulled back, only two feet from Jon's head.

"No," she cried, pulling him into the shelter of her arms.

"Leave Jess alone," Jon yelled in defiance. "You can't take her, she's Nathan's."

"Nathan's?"

"They're married."

The man started to laugh, the gun still inches from the boy. "She wouldn't marry a man, not willingly."

"She is too married. I was there. They kissed too."

When Jon said kissed Clifford's laughter died, to be replaced with a stone hard glare. His free hand shot out and grabbed Jessica by the back of her neck. "Are you married?" The words were forced from clinched teeth.

Fear deepened at the tone, but she tilted her head in

defiance. "Yes!"

"Did you give yourself to him?"

"Yes, yes I gave myself to him wholeheartedly."

His face reddened in fury, and she thought he was going to shoot her. The hand on her neck tightened. Her mind grew foggy.

"You are mine." The sharp words punctuated the mist of her mind. "You were only for me. I should've had your innocence. I knew I should have taken it long ago."

"Let her go." A child screamed, and the tightness disappeared. Jon kicked and hit. He was a fierce defender, but his blows had little effect on the man. Raker gripped him by the front of his shirt and hauled him into the air, letting him hang two feet off the ground.

"If you want the boy to live you'll get on the horse that's saddled over there."

Behind her, Sara whimpered. Jessica needed no encouragement, though she struggled to get to her feet. Never in her life had it been so difficult to get on a horse, but she finally managed. Raker swung onto his horse with ease, locking Jon in front of him with a steel arm.

"What are you doing?"

"Move."

"You need to let Jon go."

"I'll release the boy if and when I've decided you will do what you're told. You have lessons to learn about defying me."

"Please let him go. I'll go with you, just let him go."

"You can't marry me, not until I've killed the man that you gave yourself to."

"Then now's your chance."

Jessica spun in shock at the words. "Nathan!" Her jubilation was short lived as it slipped into fear of losing the man she loved.

"So you're the terror that caused Jessica to flee from her home. You don't look like much to me. Terrorizing women and using a child to get what you want. You're pathetic."

Jessica wanted to scream for him to run, but she knew it would only distract Nathan. She also knew Nathan was goading Raker. It wasn't smart to goad a snake. They tended to strike.

Raker's gun came up. Jessica screamed causing Raker's horse to shift as he fired. Nathan dove to the side, the bullet smashed into the wagon less than a foot from his head.

"Still hiding behind a boy? Why don't you get down and fight like a man?"

Jessica groaned and almost rolled her eyes, but the taunt had the effect that Nathan wanted. Raker swung from the horse with Jon still locked in front of him. The moment Raker's feet touched the ground, he tossed Jon aside. The boy flew about five feet before he hit the ground. Jessica slid from her horse, running to Jon who only seemed dazed.

"I'll kill you," Raker growled. "She was mine."

"Wrong. Jessica is mine."

Jessica gave a prayer of thanks when Raker shoved his gun back into its holster. The prayer changed to one of safety for Nathan as Raker charged him. Raker was older by nearly ten years, a little shorter but more burly. He was like a charging bull when he impacted with Nathan.

Nathan went down, rolling backwards taking Raker with him. The men were on their feet immediately trading savage blows. Jessica fought to keep from crying out as a fist caught Nathan in the side not far from where the cougar had clawed him. Though the place had healed, she knew it was still tender. The pain on Nathan's face when he staggered confirmed it, but he came back landing his own fist in Raker's face. Blood spurted from the man's nose, running down his face to join what trickled from his lips. Raker stumbled back, gulping a lung full of air.

Nathan too was breathing hard, but it was obvious now

he was winning. Taller, younger, leaner, quicker, he was taking blows, but not as many as Raker. Nathan was able to block and avoid most of them.

Jessica caught the glint of steel when it appeared in Raker's hand as he charged back in again. Raker's arm swung out in a wide slashing movement that would have sliced through Nathan's stomach if he hadn't jumped back. Nathan ducked then dove out of the way to avoid the next strike.

Coming up close to the fire pit, Nathan grabbed a piece of wood using it to block then bat away the next strike. Jessica gasped as she heard material rip, but Nathan showed no signs of increased pain as he jumped back.

She didn't realize she was crying until her vision blurred, and she reached up to wipe away the wetness. Nathan dove out of the way of the knife again, hitting the ground hard. Jessica clung to Jon to keep the boy from rushing forward, and screamed when Raker threw himself on Nathan, Raker's knife set to plunge into his chest. Nathan kicked up with his feet, sending the man flying over him. Raker rolled over the ground coming to a stop face down and stayed still.

Cautiously, Nathan got to his feet and approached the man, his body prepared for an attack, he grabbed one shoulder, shoving Raker over.

The knife protruded from Raker's abdomen. Blood oozed from the corner of his mouth, trickling down his neck. "No." The protest gurgled out, but the next word was clear, "Mine."

"No." Nathan's words were filled with certainty. "She was never yours. She was for me. She's mine."

There was another faint gurgle, then silence until a man in uniform stepped over. "Are you all right, Mr. Hawke?"

Jessica hadn't noticed the arrival, but now she looked around and saw a cluster of men. Mr. Hammond held his wife similar to how she held their son. Sara had been released from the ropes.

Jessica stood, put Jon on his feet and gave him a slight push toward his parents, not that he needed the encouragement. "Mama!" The short legs took off in a run, driving him into the arms of his parents.

Jessica followed his lead, but her steps were slower as tears and relief hampered her movements. A hand over her mouth to hold back the sobs did little good. Nathan's name came out in broken syllables, but he was already on his way to meet her.

She dove the last few feet into him. He caught her pulling her up into his arms. Her arms locked around his neck. Her face pressed into him. When he straightened, her feet dangled off the ground. She didn't notice and if he did, he didn't care. He tilted his head down, kissed her temple and cheek, and then captured her mouth when she raised it to him. Jessica met him with her own fire, devouring his essence and giving up herself for him to feed on.

"Mr. Hawke," the words finally made it through, and Nathan ended the kiss after running several others along her cheek. He eased her down his body until her feet touched the ground, but he kept her locked against him.

"Can you tell me what happened here? Who was that man? Mr. Hammond said he wasn't part of your company."

Nathan slid a hand under Jessica's chin and tilted her face up to him. "He's a nightmare that will never appear again." His hands framed her face.

He kissed her and Jessica knew it was true. Never again would she be plagued with fear of Clifford Raker. She nodded, wrapping her arms around his chest, laying her head over his heart to listen to the reassuring beat as Nathan gave a brief outline of what happened, with Sara adding details. When they were finished, there was little for Jessica to add.

Two hours later they lay in each other's arms. Raker's

body had been taken away to bury. There hadn't been much to clear up as the military men had recognized the sound of a shot over the music. They had come running, bringing the wagon master with them. They arrived in time to see Raker pull the knife. No one had shot because they didn't know the conflict, and Nathan showed he was handling it.

Jessica ran her hand gently over Nathan's chest, conscious of the bruises he had. She kissed his shoulder, reveling in having him safe in her arms. Raker had taken too much from her. She thanked the Lord that Raker's evil obsession had not ripped Nathan away from her also.

"He killed my father."

Nathan's lips brushed her forehead and his arms tightened. "I know. Sara said he admitted that to you."

"Why? What did I do?"

"Nothing, you didn't do anything. He was a sick man. I think your father saw that."

"You think he knew that Raker would kill him?"

"Yes, I think he thought that it was a possibility that he would try. I've wondered about why he would set up the will the way he did."

"Then why didn't he just send me away or we all leave?"

"Because he thought he could handle him. The will was just a precaution, a safeguard."

"I wish he'd told me. Maybe I could have done something to stop it."

"The only thing you could have done was to give yourself to Raker. Your father didn't want that of you."

"I don't think I could have." She couldn't stop the shiver at the thought. "To have him touch me like you do would have been wrong. I would have died first."

"I think your father knew that. He gave his life to protect you."

"He gave me a chance to find you." She pressed her lips to his warm chest. "Everything he gave me made it so I could find you. My father would have liked you. You're the type of man he would've wanted me to marry."

"I hope he would be pleased. I know I love your father's daughter. I'll do my best to give him a great prosperity."

"Nathan," she shifted up to look down at him. "If the baby is a boy, can we name him after my father?"

"I think that's an excellent idea." He framed her face and kissed her.

"We can have another to name after your father."

"That sounds good." He kissed her again.

"And one after you."

"What about our grandfathers?"

She smiled. "If you'd like and our grandmothers."

He was getting into it running kisses down her neck. "And I wouldn't mind a Jon of my own."

"Sara has been wonderful to me, and it's a good name."

"A very good name," he laughed.

"You sound happy."

"Oh yes. It sounds like I'll be a very happy man for a long time."

Epilogue

Nathan paused in his hammering to look out over the lush green valley. From the roof of the barn, he had an excellent view. Amos had done an amazing job picking out property. By the time they got there, he'd been able to purchase another plot of land connected to the original plots. He gave the larger, nicer of the existing houses to him and Jessica, taking the small house a quarter mile away on the other plot for himself. The only thing lacking on the property was a suitable stable for the horses, which they were close to completing.

Nathan caught sight of Amos running out of the house. Jessica had been right, he and the old man got along incredibly. Amos was talented with horses. Nathan was reveling on his fortune when he noticed that Amos had swung onto his horse and kicked it into a gallop to cover the short distance from the house to the barn. The old man, who normally was calm and unflappable, seemed in a dither when he pulled up below him.

"Nathan, that fool wife of yours has been working in the garden and baking up a mountain of food all morning while in labor the whole time. You may want to see if you can get her into bed before she has that babe in the kitchen. I'm off to fetch Sara. Hopefully, we'll make it back before the babe makes it here or you'll be delivering your own child."

With that, the man kicked the horse and sped off to where the Hammond's had purchased land about two and a half miles away.

It took a second for what floated up from Amos to sink in, then Nathan about slipped off the roof in his effort to get down. He had to force himself to take the ladder one rung at a time until he jumped the last five feet. The instant his feet hit the ground he was running for the house.

Luckily, Amos had left the kitchen door open when he left, or Nathan would have knocked it down. He skidded to a stop ready to chastise Jessica for not saying anything when he caught sight of her face. Pain filled her beautiful blue eyes as she drew in small panting breaths. One hand was braced on the work counter, the other on her extended abdomen.

"Oh, Jess." He came up behind her. "Lean back on me." He slid his arms over where their baby was working to make its way out, and rubbed. "That's it." He kissed her cheek. "Why didn't you tell me?"

"I was going to … at lunch … just …" She broke completely off with a whimper, trying to breathe.

"Relax, don't fight it. Let it come."

The pain lasted longer than he figured. The instant it eased, she sighed and slumped back against him.

"You should be in bed. But, as much as I like carrying you, it might not be a good idea. I might hurt you or the baby. Do you think you can walk?"

She nodded. "I didn't want to spend the whole day in bed. Sara said to expect eighteen to twenty-four hours on the first baby."

"I don't think you have near that long." He guided her down the hall.

"I hope so. I don't think I can make it. I was trying to be so brave."

They made it to their bedroom. "Sit here and I'll get the extra blankets. Can you undo your buttons? Then I'll help you change."

"I promised myself I'd handle this better."

He squatted in front of her and brushed back her hair in

a tender caress, "You're doing wonderful. Amos will be back with Sara soon. I'm not going to let anything happen to you." He leaned forward and kissed her. The kiss ended in an "Oh" but not from the kiss. She tightened again in pain. "Another already?"

All she could do was nod and breathe.

Nathan rose, leaned over her pressing her to his chest as he rubbed her back. Her hands locked on his arms in a vise-like grip. "That's it. Hold on to me, love. Just a little longer, it's almost over," he repeated it over and over as the pain went on longer. Finally, she sighed against him. "Have they been coming that close?"

She shook her head.

"We'd better hurry and get you changed." He fought to keep his voice calm. Inside he was feeling anything but. Pulling her dress over her head, he tossed it onto the rocker in the corner. "You won't be needing that dress for a while."

"My–"

"I know which one." He got out the nightgown she had designated and slid it over her head, letting it pool at her waist. "Let's get you situated."

"Can I have a drink?"

"I'll get it after you're settled." He slid her farther onto the bed and then placed several pillows behind her. "There, how's that?" He ran his palm over her cheek.

"Fine." She turned and pressed her lips into it.

"I'll get your water." Unable to stop himself, he leaned down and kissed her again.

He was coming down the hall with the glass when he heard another gasp.

"Oh, oh, Nathan!"

He ran to the room, shoved the glass onto the dresser, and reached for her. Jessica caught his hands like it was a lifeline of which she wasn't going to let loose.

A wave of helplessness assaulted him. He knew a lot

about delivering horses, but nothing about human babies, and this was Jessica and his baby. On Sara's last visit, she said the process was similar, but it didn't feel like it when it was Jessica in pain. He wanted to take the pain away from her, but all he could do was hold and reassure her.

After an hour, he was about as rung out as she was. With another strong contraction, her water broke. He was just cleaning it up when another contraction brought the baby's head into his hands. Then with a cry from Jessica, the shoulders made it out, and his baby slid free.

Nathan looked down, hardly able to take in the miracle he held. It was amazing.

"Nathan?"

"I have him."

"Him?"

A sharp cry pierced the air as Nathan laid their baby on Jessica's stomach. "Oh my, look at him." She reached to catch the tiny hand.

Nathan laughed as he worked to clean up his squirming son.

"Isn't he amazing?"

"He isn't the only one." Nathan leaned down and kissed her. "I love you. On the day we married, you told me that you hoped I wouldn't be disappointed. I was not disappointed then, nor am I now, and I might not be able to see the future, but I do know I'll never be disappointed that you ended up as my wife. I found my heart on the trail when I found you under those boys' clothes."

About the Author

I grew up in a small town in Wyoming loving the outdoors, sports, art, and reading Hardy Boys books. After reading them all at least a half dozen times, I started writing my own stories.

Thirty years ago I married a wonderful, honorable man. I'm mother of five children and grandmother of six boys. I love traveling. Through my husband's work and vacations, I have visited much of the United States, all over Eastern Europe, Canada, Mexico, China, Thailand, Cambodia and Australia, giving me many intriguing locations and experiences for my stories.

I am a storyteller. I write the classic hero story because I think there's a need for more heroes, love, and adventure in our lives. I'm not out to change the world with my writing; I'm just hoping to make your day a little better.

Hope you enjoy.
Alysia S. Knight

Please feel free to visit me through my website:
www.alysiasknight.com

www.ingramcontent.com/pod-product-compliance
Lightning Source LLC
Chambersburg PA
CBHW031728170626
46808CB00005B/1929